SEVEN LITTLE WORDS

Though romance writer Cathy Carruthers has been avoiding men in the wake of a painful break-up, when she meets literary novelist David Hillier neither can resist their powerful mutual desire. But her former partner is hunting her down, and her grandmother's illness means Cathy is landed with her tiny and courageous dog, Pixel. Meanwhile, David has his own problems: writer's block and the care of his father's retired guide dog. Pressures build on the couple, leading to conflict and friction — can they weather the storm together?

Books by Margaret Sutherland
in the Linford Romance Library:

VALENTINE MASQUERADE

SPECIAL MESSAGE TO READERS

THE ULVERSCROFT FOUNDATION
(registered UK charity number 264873)
was established in 1972 to provide funds for
research, diagnosis and treatment of eye diseases.
Examples of major projects funded by
the Ulverscroft Foundation are:-

- The Children's Eye Unit at Moorfields Eye
  Hospital, London
- The Ulverscroft Children's Eye Unit at Great
  Ormond Street Hospital for Sick Children
- Funding research into eye diseases and
  treatment at the Department of Ophthalmology,
  University of Leicester
- The Ulverscroft Vision Research Group,
  Institute of Child Health
- Twin operating theatres at the Western
  Ophthalmic Hospital, London
- The Chair of Ophthalmology at the Royal
  Australian College of Ophthalmologists

You can help further the work of the Foundation
by making a donation or leaving a legacy.
Every contribution is gratefully received. If you
would like to help support the Foundation or
require further information, please contact:

THE ULVERSCROFT FOUNDATION
The Green, Bradgate Road, Anstey
Leicester LE7 7FU, England
Tel: (0116) 236 4325

website: www.foundation.ulverscroft.com

MARGARET SUTHERLAND

◆

SEVEN LITTLE WORDS

Complete and Unabridged

LINFORD
Leicester

First published in Great Britain in 2013

First Linford Edition
published 2015

A catalogue record for this book is available
from the British Library.

ISBN 978–1–4448–2337–0

Published by
F. A. Thorpe (Publishing)
Anstey, Leicestershire

Set by Words & Graphics Ltd.
Anstey, Leicestershire
Printed and bound in Great Britain by
T. J. International Ltd., Padstow, Cornwall

This book is printed on acid-free paper

1

Cathy had been following the red Toyota SUV since the Dungog turnoff.

Whenever the car in front slowed on the winding road, she came face to face with the golden Labrador riding in the back. The driver was probably going to the writing workshop at Bandon Grove. He could even be the tutor. No other vehicles were traveling the deserted road this Friday afternoon.

She was looking forward to the study weekend. The brochure had described it as 'a hands-on approach to make your writing spring to life.' The chance to socialize while receiving advice from a writer as esteemed as David Hillier was simply too good to miss.

The car ahead sped up and Cathy dropped back to a respectable distance. The driver, a dark-haired man, wouldn't appreciate being tailgated. But a few minutes later, he suddenly slammed on his brakes, no doubt trying to avoid some obstacle ahead. Cathy pulled up barely a meter from his rear window, where the dog, presumably excited by the country smells, appeared to smile at her, its pink tongue lolling in a comical expression that made her laugh.

The driver gave a hand signal that he was pulling over, and she parked beside him, hoping he wouldn't say she'd been following too close. As he stepped out and walked towards her, Cathy registered his presence like a physical jolt. Yes, it was David Hillier. She recognized him from the jacket photo on his latest novel. Of course that was a publicity shot; one of those artfully casual snaps, a thoughtful pose at a desk and a wall of literary titles on the bookshelf behind him. This man was far more attractive. Tall, his dark hair windblown, he wore a black polo-neck shirt and cream chinos, casually creased. A fit, lean man, about thirty-five, he stooped to her driver's window, and sharply intelligent hazel eyes gazed at her.

'Sorry about that! It was a wombat.'

'Aren't they nocturnal?'

His sharp eyes glinted with humor. 'Whatever they are, he was taking a stroll. What about you? I presume you're not stalking me?'

His expression was good-natured, as though he enjoyed banter.

'I'm going to a writing course at Bandon Grove.'

'In that case, I'm your man. Welcome aboard.' He straightened when a volley of indignant barking reminded him of his passenger.

'Excuse me a tick. Banquo awaits.'

Banquo? Wasn't that the ghost in *Macbeth*? Even his dog had a literary name! She watched, amused, as the Labrador leaped to freedom, his leash straining as he made a determined inspection and marking of tires and fence-posts. Clearly he needed to work off energy. Checking the deserted road, his owner broke into a jog, then a loping stride, his lithe figure moving with a rhythm that suggested he was a regular runner. Man and dog reached the distant bend of the road and returned, by now both breathing faster, to where Cathy stood waiting.

'I may have to tie him up for the weekend. At least he's had a run. So you're headed for the old schoolhouse?'

Cathy nodded, patting Banquo, who was now inspecting her jeans with evident curiosity.

'It must be near here. Not much else going on.' He indicated the far rolling hills blotched by browsing cattle. 'I'm David, by the way. Course tutor. And you are . . . ?'

Cathy accepted his handshake, a natural enough greeting from teacher to student, and introduced herself. David nodded, as though he might actually have taken the trouble to examine the credentials of those attending.

'Shall we push on? I'll try not to disturb any more jaywalkers.'

'And I'll keep further back.' As she

resumed the driver's seat and followed him towards their venue, she kept remembering the warm, dry touch of his hand — a long-fingered artist's hand. Already the writing course had prospects she hadn't expected.

The deserted schoolhouse stood in a wide paddock of long grass, its porch draped with purple wisteria. David and Cathy stood at the padlocked gate, behind which two horses had ambled over to greet them.

'You don't have a key?'

David pushed back his windblown hair and shrugged. 'I suppose we can always break in.'

'Would the education authorities approve?'

He glanced down at her and laughed. 'Does it matter? I have a class to teach this weekend.'

His refusal to accept a setback was certainly attractive, but she stood firm while resorting to humor. 'I'm not in the habit of house-breaking, Mr. Hillier.'

'David, please! And you won't be an accessory to a felony. I think our problem's solved.'

Chugging to a stop was an ancient pickup truck, driven by an elderly woman. With a cheery wave from the window, she called out, 'Sorry I'm late. Jacinta overheated. I've brought the bed linen and the food.' Two gumbooted legs hovered as the plump caretaker heaved herself from the truck, gave it an affectionate pat, and opened the padlocked gate. Cathy followed David as he began to unload supplies.

'I'll help.'

'Thanks.' As he passed her a carton of bread rolls and buns, the touch of his warm hands on the bare skin of her arms made her catch her breath for some reason. He was far too attractive.

For the next ten minutes they carried boxes and bedding into the old building which had been converted to use for seminars. Cathy opened the windows in the bunk rooms while David explored the mysteries of the ancient wetback heater and the water pump.

There was something exciting about setting up house, almost like a couple on a weekend adventure, and Cathy felt a twinge of resentment when the other half-dozen participants of the course began to drift in. Oh, she was being silly today!

David Hillier was wasting no time. By five-thirty, he called for introductions and gave a modest account of his own writing background. Cathy was surprised at the varying interests of the small group when the students stated what they were writing. Isobel was working on a family history, the elderly man on a memoir of the Vietnam War. Others mentioned poetry, science fiction, a film script . . .

Cathy felt shy in the presence of such diversity. 'I'm working on a novel,' she said.

'Any special genre?' David prompted as she fell silent. She really didn't want to explain that her book, which had started as a romance, had now veered off course into a very sad account of a relationship that was over. Even thinking about that made her unhappy. If she was asked to read from her draft . . . If she even had to let him read it . . . No way! That would be like having to strip naked in front of strangers.

'No, nothing specific,' she said, expecting her tutor would raise those dark eyebrows at such ambiguity. He just nodded in an accepting way, and signaled for the next student to speak.

Introductions over, David took up a marker. 'I know you're probably hungry. So we'll make this first exercise short.' He began to write quickly on the whiteboard. 'This is just to break the ice. Half a page will do. After that, it's barbecue time and all hands can pitch in and help, okay? I'm going for a walk.'

He turned to leave but was interrupted by one of the students. 'Excuse me, Mr. Hillier. What does that sentence mean?' He indicated the whiteboard. 'It wasn't supposed to be like this. What wasn't?'

David grinned. 'Anything you like. Let your imagination run. You can use any setting — outer space, a tropical island, heaven. It's just to get the words flowing. See you at dinner, folks.' With a casual wave he was gone.

Cathy stared at the whiteboard. Already, those in the group who hadn't brought notebooks were reaching for paper and pens. A tropical island, he'd said. Heaven. Why suggest them? David was a literary writer. She was halfway through *Magnetic North*, the novel that had recently won him the Premier's Award. Terrific writing — taut, original, inevitable, but sad. A little too close to her present state of mind. She would be taking the book back to the library unfinished.

She could sense pens racing along the lines of legal pads and exercise books. Beside her, a young guy was tapping on his notebook keyboard as though possessed by devils. What on earth could inspire such a fever? She could see his tongue protruding over his bottom lip as he sat hunched, his eyes fixed above his flying fingers.

She must make a start. Everyone else was in full flow. It wasn't supposed to be like this. Seven little words. Why did she feel so apprehensive, as though at any minute something shocking would happen? No, not an alien craft landing on the roof; not a sudden car accident propelling her into the afterlife. Something closer. So close it was invading her heart. A kind of panic replaced all thoughts of completing the simple writing exercise. She would tell David it wasn't her thing; she couldn't do it. She felt intense pressure in her throat. Hastily packing her papers and course notes away, she hurried from the room, leaving the other students to glance after her in surprise.

Closing the door of the female bunkroom, Cathy lay down on the narrow bed, sighing.

You could walk away but you couldn't leave the past behind. Aaron had seemed such an interesting guy

— brainy, creative, focused. She was sporting a diamond engagement ring by the time she'd felt troubled by his obsessions. His anger flared at the smallest thing — a dripping tap, a light left on, an ornament placed at a slightly different angle. He seemed to think a woman was like an operating system; demanded to know just what buttons she wanted him to push, while she felt less and less able to respond to him. One day she looked at Aaron and realized he was abnormal. She hesitated for a moment, then added mentally, yes, she was afraid of him. Yet for a long time she had loved him, or thought so, despite his cold analysis of everything. 'You are incapable of loving!' — He'd yelled those cruel words as he tore the engagement ring off her finger.

It wasn't supposed to be like this. No, love wasn't meant to make you so unhappy. And she was going to cry again. Cathy turned her face and quietly sobbed into the pillow.

Dusk was falling. How long had she been asleep? One of her roommates must have come in quietly and changed. A cosmetic bag and deodorant stick now stood on the dressing table. Cathy unpacked a fresh top and skirt, brushed back her wavy blonde hair and applied a quick spray of Dolce and Gabbana Light Blue.

She'd been a plump little girl until her teens, when the puppy fat fell away and she grew willowy and tall. People began to say she bore a resemblance to Lady Di but Cathy had felt like anything but a princess. She'd spent those awkward years wearing flat shoes and wondering how to attract a tall boy. At twenty-five, she was more poised, yet still believed men preferred a shorter woman.

Needing a change of scenery, she went outside to the veranda. The cool air of evening would clear the exhausting emotion that always followed her bursts of grief. Four months had passed since the break-up. Shouldn't she be over it by now? The preparations everyone was making for Christmas made her loneliness worse. And writing wasn't helping. Instead of working on her novel she was filling her diary with confused outpourings. Coming to this workshop had seemed a way to get her life focused on the present, but she was far too tender to face the pain of honest writing. She would simply have to sit like a dummy, and let David draw his own conclusions as to her total lack of talent.

The perfume of wisteria saturated the fading light, where the two horses stood companionably silhouetted in the distance and David was walking with his dog. What would he say if she went to join him? She'd met him just a few hours ago. Why this strange feeling of connection to him? He'd given no hint he was looking for a relationship. In fact, he had an air of self-sufficiency, apparently needing no company but his dog. It was time to join the others in the kitchen in preparations for the barbecue. But still she lingered on the weathered veranda boards, unable to take her eyes off his distant figure.

★　★　★

It never ceased to amaze David. Ever since he'd had the good luck to win that First Novel prize, ten years ago now, people seemed to assume he had it all sorted. He could simply unlock some genie, sit down at his computer and hey presto! Another great book. If only they had any idea. *When's your next book coming out?* The question he dreaded, especially when it was his publisher who made carefully casual comments along those lines. He'd written seven novels. Of those he'd shredded three, published three and was currently trying to draft the new one. 'Trying' being the operative word. If he was having a productive day he might squeeze out three hundred words. Barely one page. And none of it was much good.

He remembered how it used to be. The creative drive would interrupt his sleep, or meals, and he'd write as though his life depended on it. Work? Could you call it that? No, it was joy, it was inspiration, it was magic . . . Now? It was more like pulling teeth; the kind of handy cliché that escaped his plodding fingers before he wearily tapped the backspace key. What the hell was wrong with him? The woman in his story — and for this book she was essential — was a two-dimensional figurehead, dead on the page, goading him with his inability to breathe life into her. One couldn't coast on back work and past glories forever. How embarrassing when the truth came out. David Hillier? Who? Just some old has-been who *lucked out* with a couple of novels.

Even worse, he was supposed to be an expert. He'd stood in front of the little band of hopeful writers who had traveled for hours to this godforsaken place to listen to him pontificate. He'd seen their willing, open faces. As trusting as that beautiful blonde girl who'd tailed his car like a lost duckling in need of a protector. Why had she made such an impression on him? And why was he thinking of her again? He'd sworn off relationships, at least while he was wrestling with the problem of his aged father and his retired guide dog. But that blonde had got under his skin, the moment he'd looked into her luminous blue gaze. Intelligent. Bright. But vulnerable. That was the impression he'd gathered from one brief glance. Who had hurt her? One would need to tread gently with her.

'Here, boy!' The obedient dog came to heel. It was time to get the ball rolling with his students. All the old plots had been done to death; all the stories were told. But how could he possibly advise them to find another job, or do anything else but write? They'd come all this way; paid hard-earned money. He didn't plan to bore them senseless with long-winded literary theory. He intended to get them out from behind desks, into situations that would test their research and observation skills. They could work on scene-setting. If worse came to worst they could all go for a good long walk.

Enough musing. He must go back and be the sociable host; establish credibility.

The sunset was now a wide sky of raging crimsons, oranges and pinks. He passed the horses, their scent mingled with earth and grass. All his senses were stimulated by this last drop of the day. Surely that was a good sign? The lovely blonde was waiting for him on the veranda, the breeze toying with her calf-length skirt as she waved, the way a woman would welcome her man home at the end of a long day. For a moment he even wished she was his woman. What was going on?

He mounted the steps. Crouching to tether Banquo to the railing, he noticed the water bowl had been topped up and an old blanket folded into a bed.

'I just thought I'd make him feel at home.' Cathy sounded nervous, as though he might not be pleased.

'That's great. Thanks. I'll bring out his biscuits in a minute.'

'He's a lovely natured dog.'

'He used to be my father's guide dog. Dad's legally blind and in a care home, so I've got Banquo.' He really didn't want to go into details; not now, with the girl standing so close, smiling down at him and running her fingers through the dog's coat in a way that almost made him envious. He was eye-level with her thigh; he could caress that finely shaped ankle encircled with its little silver chain, let his hand reach a little higher . . .

Abruptly he stood up. Just as well she wasn't a mind-reader and couldn't know how attracted he was; couldn't possibly have guessed at his unbidden surge of lust as he'd leaned close to those long, long legs.

'Time I went and washed up,' he said.

'Did you enjoy your walk?'

'Very much.'

'It's a lovely evening.'

'Yes.' She was making small talk, as though she was trying to prolong the moment. And he was in no hurry to leave either. Was that her perfume, or the wisteria? No, his life was far too complicated to get involved with anyone. He had to get his father to accept the fact that he was never going home. He had to deal with Banquo, finish the wretched book and then perhaps he could take a long trip and get his life back on the rails. By which time she'd be long gone, probably into some other man's arms. Shame the timing never worked out.

* * *

David Hillier intended to work them hard, or so it seemed to Cathy. Right after breakfast he began outlining the day's plan. She was relieved he did not ask to see the previous evening's exercise. For a couple of hours he discussed characterization, dialogue and plot, encouraging plenty of input from the class yet keeping a firm hand on anyone who wandered from the topic under discussion. Cathy watched quietly, learning from his leadership skills. He must be used to panels and discussion groups. These days, writers couldn't be solitary or shy. They were expected to perform and promote, she'd heard. That was all too far down the track for her to worry about. At the rate she was going, if she ever finished her book, she'd be an old woman in a wheelchair.

After morning tea, David considered the assembled group. 'Anyone interested in a challenge?' Briefly smiling at their blank stares, he began writing on the whiteboard:

Your character is a prospector on a 100km stretch of lonely desert road when the car breaks down. There is limited water and only a small amount of food. It is common knowledge that it is fatal to leave your vehicle. Nobody knows about this trip. Outline the character, the setting, inner thoughts and outer actions of this man as time passes.

'At least this is one problem I'm never likely to have!' murmured one of Cathy's roommates, Mary — a pale, quiet girl who wrote poetry and rarely said a word in class.

'Let's imagine you, as the author, are about to tackle this scene. Where are you?'

'Bandon Grove,' was the literal response from the war veteran, and David nodded.

'Exactly. You are sitting comfortably in our workshop, with food and drink through that door. What about if you were in the back of beyond, actually experiencing those conditions?'

'It would be real.'

'Exactly, Cathy. I had to write that scene for my last book. You must have heard stories like this. Some fellow out to explore or make his fortune; car breaks down, and he decides to walk to the nearest house. Except that's two days away. He doesn't make it.'

The class sat in silence, chilled by the story. How could anyone possibly do justice to such a painful event?

'Hey guys, cheer up! This is just a hypothetical situation. Still, from the comfort of my city home, it was just too remote. So I went there. I put myself in the place of that man and his broken-down car. I felt the heat. I saw the godforsaken landscape. I waited, and not a single vehicle came past. Apart from the fact that I could start my car and get back to civilization whenever I liked, it was easy to imagine I was truly stranded and that I probably wouldn't make it out alive.'

He smiled at their stricken faces. 'I'm not going to drop you all in the

Simpson Desert! But I do want you to be alone in an unfamiliar environment, see what your senses pick up, make some notes. Tomorrow we'll see how to transform that into a scene that has the ring of truth.'

'Is this compulsory? It's really nothing to do with my project,' Isobel, the genealogist, objected.

'Put your feet up, read my notes or a book, feel free. This is a challenge, not an inflexible order.' His cool tone changed to encouragement. 'The rest of you, take your own cars if you like. But if you want to experience real isolation, I'm happy to drop you off somewhere. It's up to you. Be ready to go in half an hour.'

He grinned at the class and walked out, leaving the bemused students to stare at the assignment he'd presented. They'd expected a pleasant weekend of literary chit-chat and advice, not boot camp.

Isobel opted to remain behind. The others took off in their own cars, having been instructed to be back no later than four p.m.; only Cathy had chosen to accept David's offer to drop her at her destination. In for a penny . . . She wanted him to see she was a committed writer. If this was how he did research, she would go along with it.

'Got your writing material? Time to hit the road.' His tone sounded approving as he looked her up and down before loading Banquo in the back.

Well, this was an unexpected bonus! A lovely day, a drive in the country, an intriguing escort. Each time David swung around a left bend in the unpaved side road, her body was thrown towards his and his bare arm made contact with her own, sending a shiver through her body. Behind her, the rhythmic panting of Banquo distracted her from her fantasy.

'How long have you had the dog?'

'Since Dad went into the nursing home. My mother died last year, and Dad went to pieces. He's a diabetic, and needed supervision.'

The fantasy resumed. Cathy imagined her fingers drifting over the curly dark hairs of his muscled forearm as the car swung around another bend. Yes! He would pull up in a shady grove, take her hand and stroke the racing pulse at her wrist. They would unbuckle their seatbelts, and he would pull her close, enfold her in his embrace, drop soft kisses on her neck and throat . . .

'What about you?' he asked. 'Have you always lived in Newcastle?'

'What? Oh — I grew up here; lived with my grandmother. I've just come back.'

'And how's that going?'

'After five years in Melbourne, I'm still adjusting.' No point in going into the whole sordid story of Aaron, or the lonely life she was leading now as she tried to rebuild her credibility as an independent woman.

'I'm a bit of a rolling stone. I like new places. Part of the territory, given the kind of books I have to research.'

'It must be lots of variety.' If only they could go on driving just like this, on and on; chatting, falling quiet, being together . . . She felt so content beside him. Surely he must notice she was sitting a little closer, leaning his way?

The abrupt jolt reminded her they'd reached the mythical desert challenge point. There was no sand, but otherwise the road was appropriately deserted: not a house, not even an animal in the empty paddocks. Just stands of blasted trees and roadside gums, and the croak of a solitary raven.

David turned to face her, his even white teeth flashing a friendly smile. Could she persuade him to stay? What if all this was a device to be alone with her? There could even be a surprise picnic in that sealed-up carton in the back. They could eat, talk a while, exchange literary gossip, and perhaps do some more personal sharing on that old tartan rug he would spread under one of the shady gums, inviting her to share a makeshift bed . . . Yes, he'd stepped out and was opening the hatch, even letting Banquo out for a walk! Cathy watched, letting her imagination soar as the well-trained dog roamed for a few minutes, then returned on command. Now David was reaching into the carton, taking out a blanket and putting it and the box on the ground. He dumped a bottle of water and a couple of apples onto the cloth.

'Supplies! You'll have to imagine the sand. No handy deserts. Ready to get writing? See you later.'

This was ridiculous. He couldn't abandon her here. The place was deserted. She had no idea where she was, or where the schoolhouse was.

Already he was in the car, fastening his seatbelt.

She felt like an abandoned child dumped outside some hospital, or left at a railway station, unwanted. Frantic, she beat the air with her hands as a cloud of midges hovered around her head. David was revving the engine.

'Insect repellent in the box!' were his

final cheery words as he drove off in a spurt of gravel. Breathing dust, she stared until the car was out of sight.

Her first reaction was anger. What kind of maniac took you into the countryside and put you out and drove away? She'd report him to the authorities who'd organized this course. This was way more than 'hands-on' learning. She'd demand her money back. She hoped they'd sack him. Who did he think he was, and what made him think he could write? She hadn't even bothered to finish his last book, never mind what prizes it was supposed to have won.

Trying to be practical, she spread the blanket in the shade and checked the box he'd left. Inside was a crumpled Akubra, a ragged long-sleeved shirt, bug spray and a bottle of tap water. It didn't take long to set up camp with those props. Within five minutes she felt she'd memorized every aspect of the monotonous landscape. Unlike everyday life, peopled with all the faces, objects and sounds that gave reality to one's surroundings, this was a place of nothingness. She could not recognize a single landmark. It was as though she'd been left on some outer planet and had no way of getting back to earth.

Her anger shifted to fear — yes, fear! What if David had an accident? What if he didn't come back? What if some stranger saw her here alone and did her harm? When would she decide to start walking back? She wasn't supposed to leave. The rule was that you must never leave your vehicle in the desert. The sun would dehydrate you, your body would collapse and you would suffer organ failure. But how could you not try to save yourself, if you knew you were alone? Sure, this wasn't a desert and she wasn't going to die. This was research. Yet the solitude frightened her. The bout of Aaron-sickness she'd suffered yesterday was nothing compared to the loneliness that now swamped her.

Defiantly, she bit into an apple. For

want of something to do, she took out the folded paper and re-read her assignment. Looking around, she made a few notes. But how could you describe emptiness, lack of human contact, nowhere to turn for help? Her thoughts drifted to the prospector. At least Cathy knew this was an exercise. Why hadn't she brought a book to read? Or her mobile phone? But that would have defeated the purpose of being here, which was to understand absolute isolation. What a state! After half an hour, unable to sit still, she paced a few meters, then realized she'd come to a decision.

Who knew when David planned to come back for her? They should have set a time to meet. If she hadn't been wearing a watch, she would have sworn she'd been there, alone, for several hours. She'd had enough of this. Time to make her own plan.

The oversized shirt at least covered her arms and hands; the Akubra was far too big, the wide brim almost obscuring her eyes. Her sandals weren't ideal footwear for this dusty, gravelled road. She had a good hour's walk ahead, maybe even two. But she'd make her own way back to the schoolhouse if it killed her, because she couldn't wait to tell David Hillier exactly what she thought of him.

2

David slowed to a crawl as he saw the weary young woman limping towards him. Draped in a long shirt and with a hat covering most of her face, she was almost abreast of the car before he was sure she was actually Cathy. She pushed back the hat and he was face to face with furious sapphire-blue eyes.

'You decided to walk back?' The fatuous words were pure instinct. He hated scenes, especially with angry women.

'What does it look like? How dare you dump me off like that!'

'You asked me to.' Stick to reason. Not working. Her contempt slammed into him.

'I asked for help with my writing. So far you've given me blisters, insect bites, a twisted ankle and a headache. Oh yes, and some stupid assignment that meant leaving me in the middle of nowhere to walk home.'

She was really upset, and he shouldn't be noticing how her high color added to her beauty. Her porcelain skin was flushed and tears trembled on her sweeping lashes. She turned to walk on, and he saw her try to conceal the limp. Maybe he could calm her down. Reaching over, he opened the passenger door.

'Here. Hop in. I've only been an hour, you know.'

His excuse seemed to redouble her fury. 'No thank you! I can find my own way home.'

What to do? He wasn't used to feeling guilty. She must have misunderstood the point of doing research the way he'd approached it for his books. He certainly hadn't meant to upset her. She was the only student who'd blindly trusted him. The others had either opted out or provided backup transport, playing it safe. Now they were all enjoying cool drinks and chat back on the shady veranda of the schoolhouse.

'Cathy!' No way was she going to walk. She plodded on, back straight, oversized hat held high.

He had to admire her. She looked so soft, but she certainly had spirit. At the same time, he sensed defensiveness — a barrier, holding him away. She was afraid of something. Or someone. A man?

If he had to pick her up and put her in the back with Banquo, so be it. Turning the car, he overtook and parked directly in front of her. He stepped out, standing so she had to face him, her expression stubborn.

'Right. That's enough, Cathy. I'm responsible for you and I'm taking you back now.'

She refused to move.

'I'll ask you one more time. Please, get in.'

'Or what? You'll make me?'

'Exactly.' He waited, prepared to pick her up and stuff her through the back door or onto the roof rack if necessary.

She suddenly capitulated and climbed in. He closed the passenger door gently and resumed his seat.

'Show me your ankle.'

Without a word she bent her knee and let him unstrap the sandal. He tested the joint where she said she'd turned her foot on a skid of gravel. Such a dainty foot, with its pretty silver anklet. His fingers probed her instep in a tender way.

'What are you doing?'

'A spot of reflexology. Each area of the body has a corresponding nerve ending in the foot. Massage there can relieve pain.'

'How do you know?' She still sounded suspicious.

'I've heard of it.'

One of his ex-girlfriends had taught him the rudiments, but he wasn't going there. At least Cathy seemed to be relaxing. Her color was softening and she'd removed the hat, setting free springy little curls of damp blonde hair. How old was she? She looked young;

defenseless, somehow, even as she carefully resumed her guard. She wasn't letting him in. But she seemed to like his ministrations.

'How's that feel now?'

'Easier. I'll put ice on it.'

He wanted to offer her some special favor to make up for the misunderstanding. Maybe she'd like to talk about her work? 'Refresh my memory, Cathy. You're writing a novel about . . . ' He was driving slower than normal, wanting her to feel safe.

'A romance. Well, that was the idea.'

'Romance? May I ask why that genre?'

She was quiet for a few moments. 'Hard to say.'

'Try.'

'Well . . . I guess I believed in romance.'

He took a bend in the road carefully. Why the past tense? She sounded defiant. 'Nothing wrong with that, is there?'

'You tell me!' She sounded so

disappointed. 'Do you know any true love stories? Everybody breaks up sooner or later.'

'Hey, isn't that a bit cynical?'

'I don't think so. My parents divorced.' Now words were suddenly bursting out from her. 'And I've split up with my boyfriend.'

'Sorry to hear that, Cathy. A recent split, was it?'

'Four months this weekend.'

Still counting the days. She must have really cared for the guy. It felt wrong to keep driving while she was pouring her heart out to him. He pulled over under a stand of scribbly gums and killed the ignition. The banked-up words flowed and her voice was tremulous.

'We were engaged for three years.'

'Wow!' Six months was the longest relationship he'd ever had. What should he say?

'See, I started my romance novel when I was still with Aaron.'

He had to strain to hear her words

over the grinding of cicadas. 'What happened?' As if he didn't know! He'd been through enough partings, but this was about her.

'See, I believed in love. I really did.'

Her voice was stronger. She sounded like it was the Holy Grail; the one thing she had to find.

'That's why I stayed so long. I thought he was different. Underneath, you know? Hoped he'd change. I can't write my book now. It's not a romance. He didn't love me.'

She was so vulnerable. He had to make this better! Don the teacher's hat. Speak gently. 'Cathy, a novel doesn't have to reflect your own life. You could still write a romantic story.'

Her crystal-blue eyes were holding his gaze, daring him to look away. 'You know that's not true.'

Did he? Unerringly, she'd put her finger right on his own tender spot. He knew damn well he was blocked right there; unable to create the real-deal love affair his current manuscript so desperately needed. She wasn't going to leave it alone.

'How can you write about something you haven't experienced? Isn't that what this assignment's about?'

'Well, yes, in a way . . . ' He hadn't said his books were fact disguised as fiction. Scenery, setting, some contemporary issue, perhaps . . . You made up the rest: plot line, and especially the emotions you'd never probed. But wasn't that exactly what a few critics had hinted at? Unconvincing female characters and surface emotions? His best work had followed the theme of man alone, contending with the elements. The women in *Iron Mountain*, *The Golden Mile* and *Magnetic North* had been peripheral. In the new manuscript, a genuine love story was intrinsic to the plot. And this girl had just reminded him he couldn't convey something he'd never experienced.

She'd fallen silent, as though drained of emotion.

He cleared his throat. 'Things will get

better. Ready to go?'

She nodded. 'Thanks for listening. I appreciate your support.'

What support? He had the feeling he'd been a jerk, but when she slipped him that shy little smile his heart did a dance in his chest. Revving up, he headed back to the workshop.

Sunday morning was to be a working session, using the impressions gathered during Saturday's research. The students would select their own storyline, write for an hour, then critique the results. Reading aloud did not appeal to Cathy, who felt exposed when anyone probed too deeply into her writing world. It was her private escape and, while she and Aaron had been together, she'd invented her romantic dreams around the strong, nurturing man she'd believed he kept hidden from the world, and from her.

Since the break-up, the hard truth of his treatment of her put paid to that fantasy. Funny, the way he'd said she was incapable of loving; he was really describing himself.

She had put distance between them. She'd moved back to Newcastle and launched her computer business. She'd thought the pain was easing. Now, this weekend was opening up the raw places. She didn't need deep thought just now. She'd be pleased to get back to her life — her work (if you could call it that), meals, and sleep.

Surprisingly, once she overcame her reluctance and started writing, the previous day's events sent her pen racing. She placed her character in an uninhabited landscape. How vividly the words came to her — the smell of dust and country grass; the mournful croaking of the raven; the undulating, empty paddocks; the irritating flies; the awful silence.

She'd covered a couple of pages when her mobile phone vibrated. Trying not to disturb the others, she hurried from the room, but the message went to voice mail.

'Is that you, Cathy? Nan here. When

you get back, dear, I wonder if you can pop in? I've had a little accident. Well, bye-bye. No hurry. I hope you're having a lovely time.'

Something was wrong. Nan's voice had sounded different. She was one of those eternally young spirits even at seventy. If she had any aches and pains she never complained of them, and the idea of birthdays made her shrug. 'I'm far too busy to get old!' Cathy had heard those words ever since she'd been a defiant young teenager, rebelling against a strict stepfather. Nan had offered her a home, not as a favor but in the spirit of a great adventure they would share together. Nan's heart was generous, with room for stray cats, unwanted dogs, free-range chickens that rooted up the plants in her vegetable garden, and even the spiders that built their swaying webs between the branches of her plum trees. It was thanks to her influence that Cathy had settled down and finished her education.

Except for her tiny rescue dog, a Chihuahua/terrier cross named Pixel, Nan lived alone now. Cathy had declined her offer to move back in. She was determined to stand on her own feet. But she visited Nan regularly, to enjoy a home-cooked roast dinner and update her on the news.

Why had her grandmother phoned? She would never interrupt a study weekend and request a visit without good reason. Urgently Cathy returned the call, but only received an engaged signal. Uneasy, she went back to class, but the flow of words had dried up. She sat for a while looking out the window or doodling, then came to a decision.

* * *

David had assigned the students' work and taken Banquo for a walk. As he strolled back, he saw Cathy waiting on the veranda, her weekend bag beside her. Evidently she was leaving. Because of him? Disappointment surged through him. Wasn't yesterday's disagreement forgotten? He'd purposely reacquainted himself with the sample chapter she'd supplied for the course, and had intended to take her aside today to offer some suggestions on structure. If he was honest, he had more than a teacher's interest in his pupil. Cathy wasn't meant to walk out of his life.

'Hello. How's the ankle today?'

'Better.' She smiled at Banquo's fervent greeting. 'Your massage and that bag of frozen peas did the trick.'

'What's with the luggage? Surely you're not leaving?'

'I'm sorry. I've been called back. My nan's not well. I need to find out what's wrong.'

'Of course.' At least she wasn't still angry with him. 'Family takes priority. I'm just sorry I haven't spent time with you privately — I mean, on your work.'

She hesitated. 'I don't think a professional writer like yourself would find much of interest in my scribbling.'

'Hey! Don't put yourself down. We

all had to begin somewhere. I had a look at your work. You have a nice way with words. The language is fresh and observant.'

'Well . . . thank you!' She tilted her head to look up at him, a soft pink coloring her pale cheeks. Her expression was confused, as though praise was a foreign concept. He had to somehow line up contact with her before she left.

'If you like, I'll read over your work more thoroughly and drop it back to you during the week.' He knew how to be persuasive. 'Just to make up for my beastly behavior yesterday.'

Cathy laughed and the sparkle in her clear blue eyes drew him magnetically. Hell, what was this? He liked women. He'd had plenty of girlfriends and several affairs that ended when his research projects took him to far-flung points of Australia. No female in her right mind wanted to leave the city life, it seemed. There were the women who wanted him to change and the ones who latched on because he was well known in literary circles and did the publicity circuit. But he'd never had anyone look at him with quite that true, genuine gaze. Surely she could see into his soul.

'Well, if you really don't mind.' She rustled through her bag and pulled out a small wad of paper. 'Here it is. My masterpiece.' He knew from her wry tone she expected criticism. Someone had done a job on the girl, that was for sure. He felt oddly protective.

She handed him a business card. 'That's me. *Cathy Carruthers. Ontime Computer Solutions*. I do residential computer support — repairs, backup, that sort of thing.'

'So that's your line of work?'

'I've had experience in the field, and my fiancé was a computer whiz. He taught me a lot.' There was that catch in her voice again. 'I'm building up a client list. It's a bit slow, but I'll get there.'

Yes, she would. She was gentle, but he'd seen a glimpse of steel in her as she limped through the heat.

'I have to go. I'm worried. My nan would never call me like this without a good reason. Will you explain to the others?'

'I'm sure they'll understand. I'm only sorry this has happened.'

Giving Banquo a farewell caress, she went to pick up her luggage, but he intervened. 'Here, let me. I'll walk you over to the gate.' Strange how reluctant he felt to see her go. Banquo seemed to feel the same. He padded after them, stopping to sniff at interesting scent trails. 'How's the weekend been? Do you feel it's been of any value, or just a waste of time?'

'Oh no, definitely not a waste of time.' She paused, then smiled at him. 'Yesterday had its moments!'

'It did! Sorry about that.'

'You don't sound a bit sorry! Though actually I think that exercise helped my writing exercise this morning.'

Was she flirting? He had to see her again. They were already at the closed

gate. He swung it open and she gave
Banquo one last pat before taking her
bag and stowing it in the car. With a
wave she drove away and he stood for
a moment, watching the trail of dust
and wishing she'd left him with the
kind of tender reluctance she'd bestowed
on Banquo.

'You lucky dog!'

The Labrador swept his tail in an arc
as though he thoroughly agreed.

* * *

Cathy drove on automatic pilot, her
mind reviewing her grandmother's
strange message. She knew Nan well
enough to interpret 'a little accident' as
an event more likely to be a catastro-
phe. A couple of times she pulled over
and redialed, only to hear the busy
signal. When she reached Newcastle she
drove straight to Sandgate, where Nan
lived alone with her pets and other
animals.

The first odd thing was the open

front door. Her grandmother would never leave an exit for her dog to wander away. At least Pixel was at home, judging by the wild volley of barking that greeted her. The agitated little dog raced to the living room, where Nan lay awkwardly angled on the sofa. Her relieved expression spoke volumes.

'Cathy, dear! How was the weekend?'

How was the weekend? How was Nan! Trust her to be thinking of everything else but herself. Now Cathy could see the reason for the busy signal; the phone had fallen off the coffee table and lay out of Nan's reach on the floor.

'What's happened, Nan?'

'Nothing important. A little fall, that's all. I'd just been to close the gate and pull a few weeds and somehow I took a tumble. I managed to haul myself to the steps and make it this far, but I'm really out of action, dear. You'll have to feed the hens, and the wild cats, and poor Pixel hasn't had a bite to eat since yesterday.'

Typical. Not a word about herself, when obviously the accident had happened on Saturday. Her grandmother had been stranded without even a glass of water all that time, and all she could worry about was chickens.

'Why on earth didn't you phone the ambulance, Nan?'

'Oh no, dear. I couldn't possibly leave Pixel by herself. You know how she is.'

'You should have phoned me yesterday.'

'And interrupt your study course, when you were looking forward to it so much? No, I knew I'd be quite all right, as long as I lay quietly.'

Cathy's mind was racing. However young at heart Nan might be, she was a seventy-year-old woman who had suffered a nasty trauma. Her cheeks were oddly flushed, her lips looked dry and there was a quaver in her voice. She was evidently weak, dehydrated and in need of medical attention. But there was no point in arguing with her. If the animals had to be seen to, best to do it immediately, and arrange transport to the hospital.

'Just tell me what you want done, Nan.'

The older woman gave a relieved nod.

Within half an hour, Cathy had fed Pixel, scattered grain for the hens and refilled water bowls. She tipped a mess of porridge and mincemeat over the back fence adjoining the swamp, where a pack of wild cats paced at the wire. She called an ambulance and gathered up an overnight bag of things Nan would need. Her grandmother looked askance at the bag.

'I won't be staying there, Cathy!' Nan would not even watch a medical show on television.

'Just in case,' Cathy said. 'No, don't get up!'

'But I must go to the bathroom! I'm in an awful state. I must be clean!'

'Just wait there. I'll bring a bucket and bowl and soap, and clean underwear.'

From the pain her grandmother could not conceal during the ablutions, Cathy knew she would be staying in hospital for some time to come. The ambulance men arrived, capable and cheerful, and Nan was transferred to a stretcher to be carried outside. It was hard to know if pain or frustration caused the tears in her eyes.

'Cathy, what am I to do?'

'Stop worrying! I'll follow you in my car. I can take care of everything here. Pixel can come home with me. As for the cats and the chickens, I'll pop in and feed them until you're better.'

'You're a wonderful girl,' whispered Nan. But Cathy knew she could not repay even a fraction of the kindness shown to her by her grandmother.

The ambulance took priority and Nan was shunted into emergency ahead of other patients, to be assessed by triage. The next several hours were a nightmare of examinations, X-rays, discussions and admission. Nan had a fractured hip and would need a pin inserted. After surgery she would be hospitalized for a few weeks, then transferred to a rehabilitation ward.

It was late on Sunday, impossible to schedule her surgery until the following day. Fretting and fuming, Nan was finally sent to a holding ward where a good dose of pain relief and a drip subdued her protests. Seeing her lie back against the pillows, Cathy knew that in her heart of hearts Nan was relieved to be in good hands. That long wait at home, alone, must have been terrifying. Remembering how she'd felt herself, on the lonely country road with not a soul to help, Cathy's thoughts turned back to David. His empathetic lesson in loneliness was one she would use in many situations. Knowing how Nan felt, Cathy kissed her soft cheek.

'Rest! I'm off to collect Pixel now. I'll see you tomorrow.'

'Thank you, dear.' Nan patted her granddaughter's hand in a sleepy way. 'She likes fish as well as meat. No big lumps. You will remember?'

Tears in her eyes, Cathy looked at the frail hand pierced by the intravenous catheter. Tucking the white cotton blanket around Nan, she left quietly, even as Nan was saying drowsily, 'Yes, cut up small, that's how she likes it.'

*   *   *

The weekend was over. Another bunch of hopeful authors let loose on the world. Naturally he hadn't told them the truth that, these days, writers were a dime a dozen and the markets were flooded already. The truth that, even if they got lucky with a publisher, they'd be tied up by deadlines and pro-motional agreements so tight they wouldn't know which way to look. The truth that today's genius was tomor-row's has-been, with a queue of ambitious scribblers happy to push in and take over at the literary luncheons, the big city book festivals, the judging panels. Sometimes David wished he'd never won those prizes and accolades

— that writer's fellowship, a finalist position in the Miles Franklin, the Premier's Award. Before that he had been just ordinary David Hillier, emerging talent, up-and-coming maybe.

In the literary world he was somebody now, but for how long? Of course those infusions of funds had been welcome. He'd been able to purchase a beach-front apartment on the site of the demolished Newcastle hospital. The history of the Royal was memorable. For 190 years the building had stood on a hill overlooking the Pacific Ocean, its itinerant users the first convicts sent to Australia, then migrants, sailors and settlers who moved to the old coal port. Now the red brick buildings had been replaced with units and penthouses taking advantage of the magnificent ocean beach at their doorstep.

David's father had gifted him with the deposit which, added to his own funds, gave him the perfect bachelor base. The place was small; just an open-plan kitchen and living room, bathroom and tiny laundry, and a sleeping loft angled to catch the morning light. He loved to open his eyes to that view, with Banquo sprawled snoring on his mattress on the floor. Luckily the guide dog had a special exemption from the body corporate's rules on keeping animals. David could do without some bunch of governors deciding what he could and couldn't do in his own pad. Their regulations annoyed him. He'd be glad to take off to research his next novel, based this time on the historic pearl-fishing industry in Broome. A tempting prospect to put five and a half thousand kilometers between himself and his responsibilities here.

Namely Dad. And Banquo. Hell! How was he going to sort that one out? His funds were almost at a crisis point. The apartment had taken all his reserves. He couldn't live on the pay from the occasional workshop. He'd have to get on and submit that grant application to the Literature Board. The deadline was only two weeks away. He'd been slow, hoping the proposed book would suddenly gel in his mind and spring to life. At present he felt there were lead weights on his fingers, slowing him down as he painfully picked his way along the lines trying to create something half interesting.

The plot line was fine. All his books had a common thread. They were set in the wilderness, parts of Australia the average person never got to see. Such places were frontier country, even now. You had to be tough to endure the climate and seasons of the Kimberley, the Pilbara or Kakadu. Men went out there for the asbestos, the gold or the diamonds as the old explorers and miners had walked into the wilds of Africa. His books had been commended for their historical research and realistic sense of place. His plots were tight, his language original.

But this time he needed to develop a woman character. An emotional woman, rounded and real, brave and crazy enough to disregard risk and accompany his main character. In his experience, when he'd talked about his research trips, females started worrying about their nail art and their hairdresser, or else their own careers in the city. He needed a character who was . . . well, just say for example, blonde, but not model-blonde; tall and slim, but not model-anorexic. He'd give her honest blue eyes, a sweetness of character, flinty resolve. A silver anklet. Obviously she'd have to be in love with his leading male. That was a laugh!

His men were easy to write. They tended to resemble himself. Not the city David in his city gear, but a man in old boots, a worn Akubra, faded jeans and checked shirt. An outdoorsman, climbing mountains, confronting the unforgiving desert, canoeing through lost canyons that had been forming during the age of the dinosaurs. Could he match up this imaginary pair?

Actually, he was feeling that throb of recognition that told him he was about to have a breakthrough. He'd pick up some takeout and go home to work on that grant application right now, while his imagination was fired up. In fantasy, you could take a willing woman with you to Timbuktu. What a pity real life wasn't like that!

A quick run on the beach with Banquo and he was settling to work when his phone rang. His father's voice roused the customary arrow of guilt.

'Hello, son. You didn't make it today?'

Sunday was David's regular visiting day. 'I was running that workshop, Dad. I think I mentioned it.'

'You did. That's right. One day just drifts into the next here. So I guess it will be next Sunday then?'

His dad's casual pretense did not fool David. Just a few years ago, Gregory Hillier had been an active man. Despite his handicap, he'd walked the length and breadth of the city with Banquo, and had kept a sharp awareness of the latest findings in his field of medical research.

A devoted husband, witty and generous benefactor, he'd been loved by all who knew him.

But, like many intellectuals, he was not good at practical affairs. His wife's sudden death had devastated him. Emotional shock aged him overnight and mismanaged diabetes led to a serious health crisis. He could neither cook balanced meals nor manage his insulin monitoring, and had been placed in a Sydney nursing home. Short term. In theory that had been the distraction to help him through the transition. Now David felt like a traitor every time he visited. His father's dim gaze would seek out his, like an orphan hoping desperately that someone would take him home and love him.

Gregory missed Banquo terribly. While he made no complaints about the nursing staff, there was one male aide he obviously did not like. He shrugged away his son's inquiry but David was suspicious. Unfortunately one heard of instances where dependent people were abused or treated like children. Such a fate was unthinkable for Gregory, who had been a respected scientist and had by now reclaimed the quick and intelligent brain his son had inherited. Sticking him away in a home seemed a poor way to repay him. Yet David was a writer; he regularly traveled great distances, and to commit himself to his father's life would effectively cancel all future prospects for his own.

★ ★ ★

He woke to Banquo's polite nudging. The dog had an infallible sense of time and David was never allowed to sleep in after seven a.m., the hour Banquo had appointed for his morning run. David pulled on his running shorts and shoes and together they crossed the road broaching the beach and set off for their jog along the sand. The ocean was a peacock blue, with rollers crashing white and frothy at the water's edge. Already black-suited surfers were catching waves while, further out, container ships queued, awaiting permission to dock and unload their cargo.

He felt optimistic. The previous evening's work had gone well. The bulk of the grant application now lay in his computer, ready for a final tweak and edit. He'd even found an hour to go through Cathy's pages and make a few notes, though romance writing wasn't his forte. He doubted he was the kind of man a heroine wanted.

Somehow this seemed a special day. On impulse he decided to treat himself to breakfast at the upmarket café near the beach. He summoned Banquo who came to heel, gazing back at the sea. A wet Labrador wasn't the ideal dog for a small apartment but David relented and gave a permission signal, at which Banquo lumbered to the water and began a dignified paddle close to shore. He retrieved a few sticks, then gave up and returned to land where his vigorous shake sent a water spray all over two passing runners.

'Had enough for today?' David had to remember that, at eleven, Banquo was considered an elderly dog despite his glossy coat and alert reactions. A bit like Gregory . . . No, not this celebratory morning. He refused to dwell on problems. He'd have the full breakfast — bacon and egg, tomato, toast, good coffee; and then he'd surprise Cathy. Arrive, just like that. Seated al fresco, the sea breeze ruffling his thick hair and Banquo quietly panting at his feet, he visualized Cathy's face when she opened the door and saw him.

★   ★   ★

The packed events of Sunday had left Cathy feeling exhausted. The transition from the workshop to Nan's accident, the hospital, the sudden responsibilities she'd shouldered . . . Even as she lay drowsing in bed, there was a dog to feed, food to provide for the cats and chickens, and a visit to the hospital pending. She liked animals, but the daily duties she reflected on would go on for months. For now, Pixel was curled against her, the tiny dog gazing up with trusting eyes. She'd had a mixed life — presumably raised kindly, for she was a friendly, affectionate creature — but before Nan had taken her in she had clearly suffered a change of owner and been neglected. Her rescuer had said she'd needed half a dozen baths to get rid of the caked filth on her coat, and she'd only accepted scraps, as though nobody had ever given her a decent plate of meat. Under Nan's ministrations she was now fully restored to health. Weighing 2.5 kg, of uncertain age but elderly by the look of her discolored teeth, she pranced like a tiny circus pony and had the heart of a warrior.

Cathy would have to go shopping to buy her suitable food. In the meantime, she had canned tuna or a sausage in the fridge. She was thinking it was high time to rouse herself and start the day when the front door knocker sounded. Pixel flew off the bed, barking in a way she presumably thought would defend the fort against infidels and black-guards. Cathy pulled on a cotton robe. Her feet in fluffy slippers, she shuffled to the door.

'Who is it?'

'David.'

Her heart literally thumped so hard she felt it shake her ribcage. What was he doing here at this hour? She looked a fright. Her hair was standing on end; she must look like Medusa on a bad hair day. This wasn't how she'd imagined it. Clutching the robe around her like a bulletproof vest, she opened the door. There he was. David Hillier. The Writer. Tanned. Handsome. Shaven and smiling.

'Well, hi!' There was nothing else to say.

3

'Good morning!'

Unimpressed by this mellow-voiced stranger, Pixel appeared intent on devouring the laces of David's running shoes. Cathy scooped her up, blushing as her robe fell open, uncovering her cleavage in rumpled teddy bear pajamas. David was laughing. Now settled in the crook of Cathy's arm, the small dog fixed her bulging eyes on him severely, her manner that of a general displeased with his troops.

'She reminds me of Flower in *Meerkat Manor*. Great show.'

Cathy laughed. It was true; Pixel did have the look and character of the brave meerkat who protected her family and stood tall against her foes. 'I loved that show too. Pixel belongs to my grand-mother.'

She had barely outlined the circumstances of Nan's accident when a peculiar wave of dizziness stilled her voice and she had to lean her body against the wall.

'Cathy, are you okay?'

She nodded. 'I must have jumped out of bed too quickly.'

How lazy he must think she was! She wasn't about to go into the details of the awful night just past. By the time she'd left the hospital and collected Pixel, it had been well after midnight. She'd tossed and turned till dawn, before drifting into a nightmare-laden sleep. Her system was simply reacting to the fright of Nan's accident, the fact Cathy hadn't eaten anything for twenty-four hours, and now the shock of her writing tutor turning up.

'Come on in.' She turned and started to lead the way along the hallway to the living room when the dizziness returned. This time David's hand was ready. Faintly she was aware of his muscular forearm and his supportive strength as he steered her into the bedroom and helped her lie back on the unmade bed.

'I'll bring you a glass of water.'

She felt too weak to worry about her appearance or the untidy atmosphere. David was back in a minute. He looked concerned as he handed her the drink.

'You haven't had breakfast?'

'No. Nothing since yesterday's lunch, actually.'

'Right! Stay there and don't move. What will it be? Eggs? Toast? Tea or coffee?'

He was adamant and she felt a great sense of relief. When had any man lifted away her burdens and said, 'I'll carry them. You rest.' Nan, her one support, was unavailable, and she hadn't realized how alone she felt.

Apparently David was used to cooking. Before long the fragrances of percolating coffee and fresh toast drifted down the hallway and her stomach rumbled. Breakfast in bed — what a treat. She had no sense that

David had any agenda other than friendship, unlike Aaron, whose gestures always had an ulterior motive. She didn't want to remember those times. He was always demanding proof that she desired him. In busy traffic he might reach for her hand and cup it around an erection she'd had no inkling of. Under a fancy restaurant's table she might feel his fingers crawling up her thigh, probing her at the same time he was talking about some computer issue. He'd seemed to think about sex all the time. If she didn't, he'd act as though she had rejected him.

Cathy shuddered at the memory, welcoming the distraction of David arriving with her breakfast. He'd even found an eggcup and set out margarine and honey in small dishes on the tray she kept in a top cupboard. She was more than hungry, she was ravenous; so intent on food that it took some time for her to register the utterly unexpected image of her writing tutor. David relaxed on the end of her bed, his long legs stretched out, munching a piece of toast as though they were an old married couple.

'More coffee?'

'Yes please.'

And he trotted off to do her bidding. Extraordinary!

★   ★   ★

David was pleased to be occupied with practical needs, which allowed him to set aside his dilemma over Cathy. Was it even ethical to think about her in the erotic way a sensuous male desires an attractive female?

Male, female? Distancing words. Hell, Cathy wasn't a doll. She was a flesh-and-blood woman, and he only had to imagine those slim hips, long legs and pert breasts to be reminded he was a horny man with instincts he'd happily indulge fully with her. Except for the pesky detail that even if he could get past the teacher/student equation, this was no time to put any more pressure on her than she already had. Clearly she was on the edge of coping.

He was in no position to step in and offer support; he had enough problems of his own. And he'd been around long enough to learn how a casual fling could turn head over heels into full-scale drama.

A few memories from recent years reared up, confronting him with images he'd rather forget. The lovely Italian, Maria, had invited him to dinner at her home — a feast attended by Mama and Papa, siblings and cousins, aunts and uncles, all making him welcome into the bosom of the family and offering a toast to the bride- and groom-to-be. And Tiffany. Amazing looks, but thick as a plank. He winced as he recalled the hysterical scene she'd thrown when he explained he was leaving to do some fact-gathering for a new book. She'd really sounded as though she'd go through with her threat to kill herself unless he married her.

No, he wasn't ready for new drama,

especially now. That was the thing about women — never mind how carefree they might act at the beginning, it wasn't long before they wanted the wedding ring and the whole bit. He certainly wasn't going down that path with Cathy.

There was some mystery about her. It wasn't hard to tell she'd only moved here recently. Her house lacked the little homely knick-knacks and trinkets which women used to make a house look like a home and not a temporary lodging. Somehow she seemed to be existing between worlds instead of putting her own personal stamp on the rooms. By the time he'd brewed new cups of coffee, she'd dressed and pulled her wavy blonde locks back into a ponytail. He thought it was a pity because he liked the way she'd looked that morning, standing at the door with her tumbled fall of hair making him think of a lover just rising. Once she was sitting at the kitchen table with her office detritus around her, she seemed to withdraw.

'So what are your plans for today?'

She ticked them off her mental list. 'Ring the hospital first. They'll probably operate today. I have to pick up groceries and food for Pixel. Then drive to Nan's, feed the chickens, make the porridge for the cats, then visit Nan . . . ' She pulled up short as David interrupted.

'Excuse me, but 'porridge for the cats?' They sit down to eat like the Three Bears?'

'No, no, they're wild! Nan gives them mince and scraps mixed up with oats . . . '

Cathy suddenly caught his image of the cats seated at a breakfast table, linen napkins neatly tied, paws grasping silver spoons as they passed around the milk and sugar. Shared laughter was a wonderful way to deal with oppressive duties. She felt like hugging him.

Perhaps he was a mind-reader. His candid hazel eyes fixed her gaze hypnotically. Cathy held the contact, a thrill of risk driving her on to seek more from this humorous, quick-witted man. She hardly knew whether to feel relieved or disappointed when David took a deliberate breath and shook himself free from that intimate moment. His voice was brisk as he drained the last of his coffee and stood up.

'You have a lot to do, and I must get home to Banquo. We'll talk about your manuscript another time.'

He was planning to walk away, just like that. She realised she had no idea where he lived, or what his phone number was. Once he was out the door, she might never see him again. She could hardly ask him out to dinner!

'How is Banquo?' The dog was the only link she could grasp before he disappeared.

'We had our usual run this morning on the beach. He'll be snoring now on my balcony, but I can't leave him too long in case he barks and upsets the other owners in the block.' He hesitated. 'Could we meet up one morning? Maybe have a swim? Introduce the dogs? Might be interesting.'

Very interesting. *Very interesting indeed*. 'Why not? Let's do it this week.' Was she being too pushy? No — he looked pleased.

'I'll give you a ring.' He tapped his shirt pocket. 'I've got your business card.'

At the door, he offered his hand with a gentlemanly openness. His clasp was firm and warm, and seemed to imprint her with an unspoken message, lingering on her skin as she watched him drive away.

She had no time to dwell on his departure. A phone call to the John Hunter hospital provided her with the information that Nan was already undergoing surgery. Cathy asked when she might visit.

'She'll be in recovery for some time. Best to ring this afternoon and see how she's doing. You can probably pop in tonight.'

That left Cathy free to cross off the other tasks on her list. Quickly she washed the breakfast dishes, her mind reflecting on the opportune arrival of David and his calming presence. Although *calming* was not the word to describe those long moments of eye contact that suggested a personal connection she found exciting. The prospect of meeting him again soon sent a pleasant thrill of anticipation through her body.

She liked everything about him — his name, his voice, his looks. Definitely his looks. That unconscious air of command. She'd seen it once or twice during the workshop when a student rambled on, disregarding the others' work, until he intervened. But he was a good listener. She'd found that out. What a new experience that had been! Why she'd confided in him she didn't know. He hadn't given her advice or offered trite words. There was nothing phony about him. Maybe that was what made him a good writer.

Unfortunately, if she was honest, her own romance book was wishful thinking; a project chosen to cover up the holes in her relationship. But she wasn't giving up. Somewhere, love existed. She knew it. And she was going to find it, even if she had to search for the rest of her life.

Pixel had parked herself at the front door as if to say nobody was going anywhere without her. Funny how much could be conveyed without language; David's last words had been matter-of-fact, yet another conversation had been taking place through looks and touch. Could he possibly be interested in her? Impossible. He was probably working hard at this very moment, tapping out another page of genius prose while she was off to cook porridge. She snapped on Pixel's lead, locked the front door and set off on her round of duties.

It was surprising how quickly one fell into a change of routine. At Nan's house Cathy saw to the animals, did a quick tidy, and packed an overnight bag of added items she thought her grandmother might be glad to have. She watered the array of plants and washed out the porridge saucepan and water bowls. With relief she looked around; the absence of Nan had changed her feeling about the house. As though a light had been switched off, a gloom hung over the deserted rooms, which already seemed to exude a dusty, unlived-in smell. The atmosphere spoke of age and infirmity. Funny, Cathy hadn't ever noticed the shabbiness of the familiar furniture and fittings. A sense of mortality depressed her and she summoned Pixel, who had taken possession of Nan's feather pillow. Glad to lock up, she headed to the shops to buy tasty morsels to suit her finicky little passenger, now seated beside her.

She found a shady space to park and partly rolled down the windows. 'Sorry, Pix, but you can't come. I won't be long.'

When she returned ten minutes later,

her carry bags laden with a few supplies for herself and a dozen samples of gourmet dog food for the visitor, she found the little dog in the driver's seat, her paws on the steering wheel as she alertly inspected the passers-by.

'I suppose you'll be wanting a driver's license and your own car next?' Cathy had to laugh out loud when Pixel pricked up her ears and appeared to nod her tiny head.

She'd missed a voice mail message while she was in the shops. She returned the call to a potential customer and set up an appointment for later in the afternoon. There was no scope for slow service in this line of work. People whose jobs depended on their hardware became very upset when a blue screen came up and 'Fatal Error' flashed across the blank space where their business records and banking details had once appeared. Cathy was aware of their distress and always presented a calm and hopeful set of options. She found the personal side of her job much more rewarding than the technical aspect.

Privately though, she could not imagine how people failed to back up and keep duplicates on a flash drive or in Dropbox. Aaron had taught her several recovery tricks, fortunately, as well as having shown her the ins and outs of various operating systems and service packages. Work was arriving in dribs and drabs, but at least it was starting. She was leaving her business cards in shops and coffee bars, and wanted to get an advertising spot in the next edition of local directories. For now she had to rely on word of mouth to expand her business.

News from the hospital was as she'd expected: Nan was in recovery and would be transferred to the orthopedic ward once her vital signs were stable. Cathy decided to do the call-out work, then pop home to feed Pixel before setting off again to the hospital. The list in her head seemed unending. One day at a time, she reminded herself. That was one of Nan's aphorisms. Funny how comforting it was to think of her grandmother's optimism and day-to-day enjoyment in life.

★　★　★

David allowed Banquo a quick leg stretch on the pocket-handkerchief section of shorn grass that edged the entrance walk to the apartments, then went straight to work on his grant application. There were lengthy forms to fill out, outlining his proposed research project. A full CV, a breakdown of proposed travel and living expenses, and a chapter-by-chapter description of the work of fiction he proposed to write were all required. Competition for funding was always intense but he stood a good chance, having moved from the Emerging Writer to the Established category. Even so, the application would stand or fall on his book précis. He was deliberately building the Australian content — the historical back story, the Chinese migrants, the unique geographical features of both land- and seascape. All he had left to develop and make convincing was the woman, a character as strong and loving and bloody-minded as those actual pioneer wives who had followed their men to the outback and endured unimaginable hardship at their side.

The picture of Cathy was vivid in his mind. He'd noted her age on the course enrollment form, not asking himself why he wanted to know. As he went back to work on the difficult content of the romance at the core of his next book, he found some of the block had cleared away. After a few mis-starts, he found the rhythm of the words and soon his fingers were flying over the keyboard, Banquo sprawled under the desk in his favored spot.

David did not appreciate the interruption when an impatient hammering on his door broke his train of thought. He sprang up to come face to face with

Mrs. Wetherby, the chairwoman of the body corporate. She was a woman who seemed to live for interfering in the peaceful lives of the other residents. In the space of one week she had posted three restrictive notices in their mailboxes. Bicycles were not to be parked in the foyer. Laundry was not to be placed out on balconies to dry. The person responsible for the raising of a tomato plant in the corporate flowerbed should remove the offending growth immediately.

She was complaining about Banquo again. 'Your dog left a trail of sandy paw prints on the foyer tiles and defecated on the lawn. Animals are banned, Mr. Hillier!'

With difficulty, David stifled the rude words he wanted to say. 'Banquo's a guide dog. He has right of passage to trains, buses, and restaurants, Mrs. Wetherby.'

And in fact to his own apartment. Further, Banquo had not soiled the grass. That matter had been attended to and cleaned up at the beach. Nonetheless, Mrs. Wetherby insisted. 'In that case, we should inspect the offending material. Unless you require a DNA test, I'm sure we can resolve the problem.'

Barely containing his frustration at such petty matters, he followed the chairwoman to the lawn, where some dog the size of Pixel had left a microscopic dropping. With much negotiation and the aid of a garden trowel, topped off by one of David's deliberate and dazzling smiles, the issue was resolved temporarily.

But as he returned to his apartment he was concerned. Technically, Banquo might be a guide dog, but he was no longer working with Gregory. A woman as persistent and as negative as Mrs. Wetherby might find a legitimate way to get rid of the aging pet who had given his life in service and affection. Even now, Banquo was lumbering out from under the desk, his heavy tail whipping to and fro. Cords and plugs were hanging from his head and tangled around his paws as he padded to greet David as though he'd been absent for a week.

'Banquo! No! Stop! Don't move!'

It was too late. There was a flash, a crash, and the laptop lay face down, keys shaken loose, its screen a hopeless emptiness.

★ ★ ★

Cathy was about to leave for her house-call job when David rang. He sounded very concerned as he explained about the accident.

'I don't know what to do. All my work's just gone.'

'I'm sure it's there, David.' She slipped into her professional soothing mode, although until she assessed an individual crisis it wasn't possible to know. 'As long as you saved the work . . . '

'That's the problem. This bloody woman came banging on the door and I think I just went straight over to shut her up.'

Cathy smiled a little. The suave author had changed to an angry, upset male who'd lost his most precious asset. Helping was second nature to her, especially when in this case it was the perfect excuse to see him again before the day was over. She paused. The logistics were difficult with Pixel, a job to do and a visit to Nan already penciled in.

But David was evidently desperate. She'd manage somehow, even if she had to stuff Pixel in her computer repair kit and smuggle her into the hospital.

'I have a job booked, David. It's simple enough; just a transfer of data to a new hard drive. How about I call at your place late afternoon? Is it okay if I bring Pixel? She hates being alone.'

'Cathy, bring a Great Dane if you like. You'll make me the happiest man alive!'

It was just a turn of phrase, she knew, but an involuntary smile touched her lips. 'That's nice!' She was aiming for a light exchange, and did not intend the wistful note in her tone.

'Just one thing.' He'd evidently had a last-minute thought. 'Can you pop her in a basket? We have a resident witch here. She eats puppy dogs.'

'Sure.' She had no idea what he was referring to, but it wouldn't worry Pixel to be hand-delivered like royalty, in a litter. Making a note of David's address, she decided on a change of dress and made up her face with more care than she'd planned.

David's apartment was certainly in the expensive part of town. Newcastle East had changed enormously since Cathy had headed south to settle and work in Melbourne. The old hospital, for all its views, had been utilitarian — a sprawling red brick tower of squinting windows. A couple of wings had been retained and now the remainder of the land had been developed as upmarket residences. A green and rolling park, a fountain, shade trees and open spaces had magically appeared, along with the kinds of restaurants and eating places that oozed high living, service and a seriously high bill.

She was surprised David had opted to live here. She'd had a romantic idea he was a wanderer, never tied to a mortgage or a nine-to-five desk job. From his books, he seemed to project a carefree spirit. She rather fancied that life herself. Australia was such a vast place, in parts as weird and unique as the planets of outer space. Yet most people worked their entire lives, eventually dreaming they would buy a motorhome and see the country. But how many really did that? Unfortunately, along with retirement came old age, with its infirmities. David's parents and Nan were proof of that.

Reminding herself that responsibilities could occur at any age, Cathy gathered the dog and found David's apartment, where a very subdued Banquo lay banished on his mattress in the corner. Any worry that he might attack the smaller dog was put to rest as Pixel, freed from her carrier, immediately bounded up to him and nipped his nose, adding a few yodels and brays to advise him she was a force to be reckoned with. Banquo lay even lower, his big head dejectedly cast down on his paws.

'Poor old fellow! Surely you're not punishing him, David?'

'He's punishing himself.'

'You mean you left those leads and cords on the floor in that appalling mess, and then you blame him for this?' She indicated the results of the accident, spread across the desk. Fingering the dislodged keys and dead screen, she looked doubtful. 'Oh dear. Not good. All I can suggest is fitting an external keyboard tomorrow. That way I might be able to see what's retrievable; if need be, get an analogue of the disc created. But you're up for a new computer, I'm afraid.'

'Not what I need right now. I'm

cash-strapped, to put it mildly.' He saw her surprised look. 'You thought I was wealthy?'

'Not exactly that. But those prizes, and the book sales . . . '

'Oh Cathy, you have a lot to learn about the writer's path. It's a feast or a famine. Emphasis on the latter. And it's my own fault for putting all my savings into this place.'

'Why did you? This place doesn't seem quite like you.' She hoped he wouldn't think her intrusive, but he seemed happy to talk.

'I had a few different ideas at the time. There was a girl, for one thing. Talk of settling down. And my parents were in the city. Mum was a live wire and she managed Dad's diabetes and kept him on his toes.'

'What happened?'

'In a nutshell, everything collapsed. The girlfriend moved on. Mum simply went to bed one night and didn't wake up. Massive coronary. And Dad went to pieces. With his minimal vision, he was hopeless with cooking and seeing to his medications. Eventually he went into a diabetic coma. Thought I'd lost him, too. I'll never forget taking that phone call. Well, you'd understand, given your grandmother's accident.'

Cathy nodded. 'Yes. It's been a hard year. Obviously for you as well.'

When her soft tone conveyed empathy, he gave her one of those penetrating looks that saw into her heart and invited intimacy. 'Wounded warriors, eh?' David seemed suddenly uncomfortable with the moment of intimacy. 'I've prepared a snack. Fruit juice okay to drink?'

She'd noticed he had a way of pulling back like that. All at once he was the charming host, producing paté, hummus and crackers, along with the jug of apple juice he took from the fridge.

'This should see us through till dinner, anyway.'

'Dinner?' There'd been no mention of her staying for a meal. She'd planned to visit Nan and head straight home, but when she said so he looked concerned.

'I think the least I can do is cook you something, Cathy. No more skipping meals, okay? What time are you going to the hospital?'

She checked her watch. 'About now, actually. I'm not expecting to stay long. Nan will be drowsy, so it's just to reassure myself.'

'Tell you what. Leave Pixel here, see your grandmother, come on back for a quick bite to eat and you can still be home and tucked in by nine o'clock.'

The plan appealed. The two dogs had quickly established that they were equals in heart if not in size, and lay peacefully side by side on Banquo's mattress.

'Spaghetti bolognese acceptable?'

'Anything at all.' She couldn't deny she felt a frisson of excitement at the thought of sharing a quiet dinner for two with him.

Cathy had seen enough medical shows on TV to imagine the operation her grandmother had endured. Bone surgery was an assault on the body. But as she found her way to the orthopedic ward and entered Nan's cubicle, she was deeply upset. It was hard to recognize her grandmother through the tangle of leads, tubes and machinery she was attached to. Blood and some clear liquid dripped from bags suspended from the IV pole beside her bed. A cardiac monitor steadily beeped. Superficial scrapes and bruises she'd sustained at the time of the fall and during her painful journey back to the house scarred her wrists and hands. A catheter bag was measuring urine output and an oxygen mask lay askew, as though she'd restlessly pulled it from her face. Some kind of cradle hidden by the cotton blankets protected the injured leg.

'Hello, darling.' Gently Cathy bent down and kissed the inert form, but her grandmother was still groggy and did not speak. Her blue eyes fluttered open briefly and she pressed Cathy's hand. In silence, Cathy arranged toiletries and nighties in the bedside table.

'Are you in pain?'

She could not make out the mumbled answer but guessed some pretty strong medication must be on board. At least there was no evidence Nan was suffering.

Feeling helpless, Cathy sat beside her for a few minutes. The impact of the accident was hitting home to her. You coped, in an emergency; of course you acted like a pillar of strength. You had no time to think about yourself. Now, sitting beside one of the most significant people in her life, Cathy saw how a simple accident had made Nan weak and dependent. Would she ever be the same again? The thought frightened her. Aaron was gone from her life. Her mother lived in Germany now, with Cathy's stepfather. Who else could Cathy turn to in her own hour of need?

A nurse wearing navy trousers and a white and navy tunic stepped into the cubicle and inspected the infusions. 'No need to go. I'm just checking vitals.' She placed a thermometer in Nan's ear, counted her pulse rate and wrote the findings on the chart. Efficiently, she calculated the flow of the IV bags, straightened the oxygen mask and lifted back the blankets to examine the circulation in the extremities of the injured limb. Replacing the covers, she smiled at Cathy. 'She's doing fine.'

'But she seems so . . . '

The nurse was used to this ward. 'They're all pretty much like this when they return from surgery. In a few days you'll see a big improvement.'

'How long will her recovery be?'

The nurse gave a shrug. 'She's elderly. Some of them never fully recover. The break's been pinned. The leg will need to be rested while it's healing. Then there'll be rehab. A physical therapist will work with her, plan specific exercises, maybe aquatic therapy. If she lives alone, they won't send her home till she's walking without support. That's three months minimum . . . if at all.'

A call bell was ringing from a curtained cubicle by the window. The nurse went on with her duties. Nan was clearly sleeping off the anesthetic. There was nothing Cathy could do for her, yet she felt like a deserter as she slowly walked away, trying to digest the nurse's information. A moment's inattention, a simple stumble, and Nan's life might be changed forever. It was an awful price to pay.

*　*　*

David was going to an inordinate amount of trouble to prepare his simple dinner.

The evening was mild enough to eat out on the balcony, which was protected from insects by a transparent awning. He set the small table there with a checked cloth, made sure there were no spots on the silverware and glasses, and cast a glance around the apartment for a centerpiece, selecting a very unusual camphor laurel paper-weight he'd bought on one of his trips. As he mixed a French dressing for the salad, his mind was on the young woman who, less than a week ago, hadn't existed in his mind.

Every time they met, his respect for Cathy grew. She might be ten years his junior, yet she showed a strength and responsibility he had to admire. What had he been doing when he was twenty-five? Trekking around the country, enjoying on-and-off relationships, barely remembering to send his parents a card at Christmas time. Oh, they'd been proud of him! His first published book, an unexpected success, placed him squarely as an up-and-coming writer. His mother, a lover of the arts, praised him and forgave his lapses. Gregory, equally admiring, had been busily publishing a number of research papers in scientific journals and naturally considered David a chip off the old block.

Neither parent drew attention to

their son's less admirable traits such as his wandering nature and his lack of commitment to the women he so easily attracted with his good looks and famous name. Here he was, at thirty-five, barely juggling the things Cathy accepted as her duty. She took respon-sibility for her life — was running a business and studying to develop her writing skills — yet was willing to drop everything and care for her elderly grandmother. On top of that, she had gone out of her way to help him, arranging to lend him a portable keyboard while she attempted a retrieval of his lost application.

Why? She had no ulterior motive he could see. She was simply a helper, willing to give of herself. And he knew that someone had taken advantage of that fact; probably the other half of that relationship she'd left. He didn't think she was the kind to walk away without good reason. Despite her humor and her ability to stand up for herself, he sensed she'd been hurt. Indignant on her behalf, he found he was chopping the salad vegetables to a pulp. Cathy deserved better.

Better than David. It was madness, thinking he might woo her. For he sensed she would respond. They'd shared a couple of moments when it would have been too easy to step into each other's arms. He'd held back; he had to. In a few months he'd be headed west, to Broome. Her life was here with her work, her Nan, and the host of animals she willingly cared for. He couldn't tell her that she was the heroine in his storyline. He'd found his romantic ideal. What a pity Cathy could only be a character of his imagination, the ideal woman of his dreams.

She must be here. Pixel was already at the door, her tail whirling like a Catherine wheel as she welcomed home her stand-in slave.

4

In the eaves, pigeons warbled softly. Lost in a dream, her eyes flickering in REM sleep, Pixel was fighting some imagined antagonist as Cathy opened her eyes and lay absorbing the sounds of an early summer morning. The ticking of her bedside clock drifted out of awareness as her thoughts wandered to recent days.

From the chaos of a week ago, a routine had evolved. As the nurse had predicted, Nan was making an excellent recovery. The catheter and IV lines had been removed; she was eating normally, and was usually sitting in an upright chair when Cathy visited. Naturally Nan had made friends with the other patients in the four-bed room. She regaled her granddaughter with anecdotes about their health and families, and seemed to know all their pets by name, while Cathy reassured her that her own animals were well looked after.

Most days there'd been some reason to call at David's. Perhaps that was why she now snuggled lower in the warm bed, smiling to herself as she recalled snippets of their time together . . . the dogs trotting along the sand; David proudly serving up his home-made curry and rice; his gratitude when Cathy managed to recover his lost work. The activities were everyday enough.

Simmering, though, was that connection she felt, responding to a casual brush of hands or moment's closeness as they sat side by side at his computer, re-setting programs. He'd been able to postpone the purchase of a new machine, thanks to her loan of the spare keyboard. To celebrate, he'd insisted they go for a drink at the bar of the upmarket restaurant nearby.

Cathy wasn't a stranger to such venues. Aaron had made a point of dining out at the most expensive and exclusive food outlets in Melbourne. But how different those awkward meals had been. She reveled in the easy laughter she and David shared as they sat at the bar, Cathy balancing a tall glass of a delicious creamy concoction, its sugared rim decorated by a figurine of a flamenco dancer. David sipped red wine. The discreet lighting and the background cocktail music from the performer at the Kawai grand piano created intimacy, and as they stood up to leave, David's hand casually cupped her elbow. Outside, they crossed the sloping park at sunset.

It would be fully dark in about an hour. At present, nesting birds were silhouetted against a vibrant sky as they arrived to settle in the generous spread of branches overhead. Scattered frangipani flowers lay like fallen candles on the grass. David picked one up and tucked it behind her ear. 'Beautiful', he'd murmured, and she was not sure whether he referred to the flower or to her.

He seemed restless as the sea wind ruffled his dark hair. 'Know what I really fancy?'

Her senses were responding to the night air, the warm breeze, the rolling of the surf . . . She knew exactly what she fancied, as she noted his firm mouth and hard jaw stippled with the day's growth of beard.

'What?' She kept her thoughts to herself.

'A swim. It's the best time, just before dark. How about it?'

She had no swimsuit, and wasn't planning to skinny dip on a public beach. But he had made up his mind.

'Come with me anyway. The dogs will be fine for a while. I really need to burn some energy.'

She almost smiled at her immediate thought. She really had a one-track mind tonight! 'I don't mind watching,' she said. 'It is a lovely evening.'

A short walk took them towards the growing sound of surf, the breaking rhythm as regular as breathing. The sand was cooling when she slipped off her sandals and walked barefoot beside him. Without waiting, he stripped off his shirt and pants and, wearing only his low-cut boxers, waved and ran ahead into the water. Beyond the breakers he struck out along the beach in a crawl stroke, his strong rhythm suggesting that swimming must be a regular pastime.

Far along the sand he swiveled to catch a few waves, body-surfing towards shore, then heading back out to face the steady rollers as they folded into foaming crests. His figure was growing indistinct as the light went. The horizon line had darkened, underlining the fading apricot ridge of the night-grey sky. The far ocean was navy blue.

Cathy sat watching the pale moon and the pulsing of the closest star, Venus. Wasn't it the ruler of love? David had backstroked towards her and was leaving the water now. He stood outlined against the backdrop of sea and sky and Cathy caught her breath as he strode up the beach, water streaming from his strong chest and tapering hips. For a moment he had the look of an archetypal god, the original work of art. He was close enough now for her to notice his sleek wet hair, the droplets sliding from his dark chest hair and puckered nipples. His low-slung shorts, dragged down by seawater, stayed up only by some miracle and she had a daring impulse to peel them away and reveal the whole man in all his beauty.

'How was it?' As if she needed to ask! His white teeth flashed.

'Refreshing.'

'Lovely,' she'd responded, thinking of him. Of course she'd seen images, statues. Michelangelo's masterpiece was a David, too. But she'd never thought it possible to respond so deeply to a flesh-and-blood man.

Still the pigeons cooed. Pixel's dream had passed and she lay fast asleep, curled at the end of the quilt. Lost in memories, Cathy sighed, allowing her fingers to trail over the soft contours of her breasts. She felt their rounded nipples peak and harden, sending a quick shaft of desire to clench her womb and make her draw an involuntary breath. She reached down then, under the covers, while in her imagination David's penetrating eyes looked down into her own, and his warm mouth came closer, claiming hers.

★　★　★

Nan's convalescence wasn't all plain sailing. She was counting the days of her hospitalization, and seemed to discount all advice that she would not be going home for months. As she became restless, she vented her frustration on Cathy.

'Did you move the laying hens to the wire enclosure?'

'Yes, Nan.'

'What about the litter of wild kittens? Have they been born?'

'Yes, Nan.'

'And my African Violets — you're not

getting any water on the leaves?'

'No, Nan.'

Her moods were understandable. Cathy was worried enough about her grandmother's future; how must Nan feel? Unless Cathy agreed to be her caregiver, there might be a real breakdown in their closeness. Nan wouldn't go quietly, into a home or anywhere else.

Cathy discussed the problem with David. He was having somewhat similar issues with his father. Christmas was barely a fortnight away and the reminders were everywhere. Carolers had been to Gregory's nursing home and he was demanding to know where he was to spend Christmas Day.

'It can be an awfully lonely time.' Cathy had nothing planned and was already anticipating the grim prospect of waking up alone on the festive day. 'I found a flyer in my letterbox, inviting solitary people to attend a charity lunch. I even thought I might go.'

David didn't laugh. 'I've nothing

lined up either. What about this for a plan? We'll take both dogs to visit. Your Nan can be wheeled out into the hospital grounds. Then we'll drive to Sydney and see Dad.'

'Brilliant!'

'That takes care of the day and makes everyone happy. That includes me, Cathy.' His look told her he wanted to spend the day with her. If only he would come out and say it!

'I could pack up a picnic to have on the way. A visit from Pixel will really cheer Nan.'

'And the same with Banquo. He and Dad deserve to be together.' His face clouded. When he traveled, alternative arrangements awaited the guide dog. The fate of elderly dogs was not something he wanted to dwell on. It seemed that once a certain age was reached, your usefulness was forgotten and you were unwanted. And that went for humans, as well as animals.

The time before Christmas was passing swiftly, with a rush of computer-related work that kept Cathy driving from one boundary of New-castle to the other. Her mobile rang early in the morning or late at night, as though people assumed she had a rostered staff available twenty-four hours a day. One call rang to her landline at eleven p.m. She was already showered and half-asleep, but stumbled out of bed to take the call.

'Computer repair service,' she said, a frown creasing her brow as she remembered that her business card only listed her cell number.

'Hello, Cathy.' The familiar voice sent a shiver of disbelief through her. Aaron! How did he know her home number? And why was he calling?

'I thought I'd let you know my plans for Christmas.' He sounded chatty, as though they were still an item.

'Christmas? Why?'

'We haven't finalized arrangements. Mum wants to know what time we'll be driving out for dinner.'

'Aaron! Listen to me. You know it's

over. We broke up. You have the engagement ring.'

He actually laughed, as though she was joking. 'That's no problem. You can have it back.'

'Aaron! I don't want a ring. We are not together. Don't you understand? It's over.'

Again he discounted her words with a laugh. 'Come on! Don't be difficult, Cathy. Mum needs to know. Should I tell her seven p.m.? Or earlier?'

She was pulled back into her past with a man who never seemed to understand her.

'You know it's what we always do.' His last words sounded anxious, as though he couldn't cope with a change to routine. Well, he would have to this time.

'Listen to me, Aaron. I don't know how you found my number, but I'll get a private line if you ring me again. I don't want to see you. I hope you move on; I hope you meet someone nice. But it's not me. Don't phone me. I'm going to hang up now. Goodbye, Aaron.'

She slammed down the phone as though it was a bomb, her hands trembling and her legs shaking. She knew Aaron was strange. Even so, to track her down like this, and to talk as though they'd simply had a minor tiff . . . He really was odd. What if he found out her home address and came after her? She had heard about stalkers . . .

It was impossible to go back to bed as though nothing had happened. Perhaps a cup of hot milk, something to nibble — anything to restore her shattered peace of mind. Options raced through her mind. She could move. Change her number. That would wreck all her efforts to resettle and get a business going. Perhaps she'd got the message through to him this time. Hopefully he would leave her alone. Fortunately he was in Melbourne, nearly a thousand kilometers away. She only wished he was on the moon.

Carrying her cup of milk, she went back to bed and was grateful for Pixel's

111

company as the tiny creature cuddled affectionately into the crook of her knees. It was impossible to sleep. She picked up a magazine and riffled through the pages. The annual horoscopes were predicting the coming year and she read the outlook for Virgo. With luck she'd find good news. The past year had certainly had its upsets, and Aaron's reappearance would have to count as the worst. She slept at last, but her dreams were uneasy.

★ ★ ★

She took the magazine with her when next she went to the hospital. Her work schedule, combined with all the animal needs, had kept her busy until late. For once it was easy to find a parking space. There were few people in the entrance area where in the daytime visitors could buy refreshments, toys and pharmacy items. Now, Cathy was reminded of a fairground after closing time. Metal grilles obscured the cafeteria and shops.

A cover lay over the baby grand piano, where volunteers sometimes introduced a note of pleasure into the hospital setting of sickness and suffering. As Cathy walked along the muted corridors, she passed wards with signs denoting the nature of the varied illnesses that brought people into hospital.

Waiting with Nan that night in emergency, she'd been drawn into the drama of ambulance arrivals, gurneys bearing injured patients, and distraught parents nursing flushed and crying toddlers. Now she was walking past wide doors labeled hematology, urology, and cerebro-vascular. The human body was heir to such a range of sicknesses. Acquiring enough knowledge to diagnose and treat them all intrigued her. There must be hundreds of professionals at work within this big complex. Occasionally she passed a hurrying nurse, a doctor with the inevitable stethoscope slung around her neck, or a patient heading outside to sneak a forbidden cigarette.

On her way to Nan's ward, Cathy paused by the elevators to read the floor plans. Somewhere above were operating rooms, delivery suites, and outpatient and mental health facilities. The hospital was a self-contained world. Cathy felt a compulsion to know more. Fixing computers was one thing, but what would it be like to study the intricate human body and heal its problems?

Nan's face lit up with relief when Cathy walked in and stooped to kiss her. 'Where were you? I've been worried.'

'Oh Nan! I was working. I had to drive out to Maitland on a job, then double back all the way to Stockton.'

'Did you see to the animals?' Nan sounded doubtful.

'Of course!'

'I don't mean to fuss. But I lie here all day, worrying. I thought I'd be home by now.'

'Haven't they talked to you about that?'

'Some silly girl suggested I'd need to go to be rehabilitated. You'd think I was a drug addict! I soon told her I'd do no such thing.'

'You might have to.' If Nan was going to be obstinate, Cathy would have to put her foot down. She was not going to attempt to nurse her grandmother back to health. If Nan needed physical therapy, she would have to accept the fact.

Changing the subject, she pulled out the magazine she'd brought. 'I was looking at our horoscopes,' she said. 'Want me to read out Virgo?'

She and Nan shared birthdays only a couple of days apart. Perhaps that was why they related so easily. Helpers, worriers, self-effacing yet amused by life's ironies, they shared so many common traits. Her grandmother brightened. She was a firm believer in the stars, ever since having her own horoscope professionally drawn and interpreted many years before.

'Yes. We'll see what's in store, Cathy,

shall we? I know these magazine horoscopes are superficial, but even so . . . '

Cathy laughed and read aloud:

This year you expand your mind through extended study. There is the possibility of a sea change for many Virgos. Be ready for changes to your living arrangements. You're on a mission to inject more fun and romance into your life. As you give out to others, just watch as it comes back to you.

'Fun and romance!' Nan's laugh caused the patients in the opposite beds to stare. 'Well, that will certainly be a change.'

'For me, too. I'm not sure I could cope with another sea change.' Cathy folded the magazine in the bedside drawer. 'I'll leave this,' she said. 'You'll enjoy the Pet Corner photos. By the way, the brown hen is clucky. I made her a nest and she's sitting on a batch of eggs in the washing basket.'

'They'll hatch after twenty-one days. Just in time for New Year. I'll be home for sure.'

Cathy did not reply. But, as she was leaving, she stopped at the nurses' station and asked if her grandmother could be seen by a counselor or social worker. It would take more than Cathy's advice to keep her in hospital until her hip had mended. The memory of David's plan cheered her. A visit from Pixel on Christmas Day would be exactly what the doctor ordered.

She'd thought of collecting Pixel and meeting David for a beach stroll, but as she left the hospital the street lights were already on. Parking outside her house, she sat for a moment, trying to still the uneasiness she felt. Aaron's call had upset her far more than she'd expected. Her worst doubts about him had been stirred up by his peculiar phone call. He'd sounded completely rational, to the point where Cathy almost doubted herself. Had she not made it quite clear they were over? What else should she have said or done? If he'd suddenly emerged from the front door and waved, she wouldn't have been surprised.

With growing apprehension she went inside, grateful for the riotous scolding of Pixel, who clearly did not appreciate her vigil alone at home.

'Sorry, little Pix! I know it's past dinnertime. I had such a busy day.' Now she was chatting away in an empty house. Who was crazy? Aaron, or herself?

Moving instinctively, she dialed David and felt a surge of gratitude at the sound of his voice. 'Are you busy?' Her heart was thudding; she felt there wasn't enough air to breathe.

'Not really. I was about to ring you, actually. I thought we might get together over your manuscript.'

'Tonight?' He couldn't know he was throwing her a lifeline.

'Sure. Why not? My place or yours?'

She couldn't face returning a second

time to her deserted house. 'Can you come here? Pixel's been alone for hours. You can bring Banquo if you like.'

She heard him chuckle. 'Dogs! It's as bad as having kids, I'd say. See you soon.'

David was coming. For a moment tears of sheer relief came to her eyes. So she was being ridiculous. She just felt invaded, and all the confusion and hurt of the break-up with Aaron was threatening to overwhelm her.

But David was coming. She was safe. The words were like a mantra she kept repeating in her mind as she fed Pixel and made herself a quick sandwich, standing at the bench.

* * *

Something was wrong. He just knew. Intuition. Without bothering to change or spruce up, he grabbed her pages and Banquo's lead, and within fifteen minutes he was pulling up behind her white Corolla. There was the usual volley of barking when he knocked, and Banquo whimpered happily. There was a skitter and scamper of paws as the friends sniffed noses and nether regions with doggy protocol.

Cathy looked tired and drawn.

'Hard day?' Her nod affirmed his guess. 'Want to tell me?'

'Later.'

'What, then? Straight into the writing?'

Unusual. She didn't offer to make tea or coffee. Hadn't a word to say. She just came and huddled beside him, quite silent.

'I thought we could talk about your structure. There's a lot of backstory in the first chapter. I think it would be better spaced out; maybe partly converted to dialogue.'

She wasn't paying attention. Just sat there, face serious, picking at her nails. Only the dogs were normal, Pixel perched now on Cathy's lap and Banquo clattering a plate around the kitchen floor as he licked at non-existent leftovers.

'Listen, if you're too tired for this?'

'It's not that. I've had an upsetting phone call.'

'Some pervert?'

'No. Aaron. He knows where I am. He thinks we're still together. He thinks we're going to see his family for Christmas dinner.'

She was like a frightened child in need of comfort. How did one do that? His former girlfriends had stirred up plenty of emotions, including desire, admiration, lust, irritation, and that trapped feeling. He couldn't ever remember this feeling of concern. His women had played a role in his life — a foil to his intelligence, competitor, someone to impress. None of them had acted like Cathy — as a helpmate, and as a friend.

Here he was, the writer, at a loss for words. Cathy had a cool, objective eye. She would recognize false reassurance. He needed the other language. Eye to eye. Body to body. The silent communication of touch. Gently, very gently, he pulled her upright and held her, his arms enclosing her, his touch stroking her back, erasing her worry and her hurt. His fingers strayed soothingly through the rich waves of her hair.

'He said I am incapable of loving.' She spoke against his neck, her voice so quiet he wondered if he'd heard right. Incapable of loving? She, who gave so easily, caring for her grandmother, for Pixel, for the horde of unwanted cats and rummaging chickens? For his lost work. For him.

'Cathy!'

'Yes?' She was very still, standing there, light and pliable and yielding against him.

'You are a very loving woman. Anyone who tells you otherwise is . . . a fruitcake.'

'What?' She lifted her head. 'I thought you said a fruitcake?'

'It's an old saying of my dad's.'

'I've never heard it.' There was just a

flicker of a smile there, lifting the corners of her vulnerable mouth.

Very softly, very carefully, he bent his head and placed a cherishing kiss on her soft lips, almost immediately moving back, not taking advantage in case she might misread his gesture, and in case he gave in to his impulse and let that kiss be more — the deep kiss he really longed for.

★   ★   ★

The tension eased after that. David put the kettle on, Cathy opened a packet of shortbread and they had supper, dropping crumbs the dogs snapped up before they hit the floor. Cathy brought the conversation back to Aaron without sounding that note of panicky worry.

'As long as he leaves me alone I'll be okay.'

'I'm sure he understands now. Maybe he really did think you two just had a lovers' quarrel.'

'Some quarrel!'

But she let the topic drop. He stayed for an hour, chatting about their Christmas plans and moving on to share a few travel adventures. The memory of their kiss kept intruding, and reluctantly he summoned Banquo.

'I'm getting too comfy here. Better get rid of us now or you might have two extra guests in the spare room.'

'I haven't got a spare room.' She smiled and blushed a little, thinking perhaps, as he was, of the queen-sized mattress in her bedroom.

'Me neither.'

She seemed to be standing around at the front door, delaying the moment. What would she do if he kissed her again? Properly? It wasn't the right time. Tonight she needed tenderness, not passion. He just placed a finger under her chin, lifting her face.

'Goodnight, sweet Cathy.'

With Banquo at his heels, he left her quickly, before he gave in to temptation. She was still standing at the front door as he revved the engine and turned the car.

Poor Cathy, caught up with a guy like Aaron! The conflicts of romance, love, desire or plain lust were beyond him. However it began, there was always a point in the end when the charm of novelty faded. The eyes of his current woman would look into his with a changed expression. He knew that look! *What about me? My rights? My life? My career?* Oh yes, he knew the way that soft eyes grew steely and warm flesh pulled away. *Do you really expect me to throw aside my life and follow you to the back of beyond? If you loved me . . .*

And then, of course, the big scene was next. Because his back was against the wall and he wasn't a liar, he told the truth. No, Rachel (or Heather, or Tracey, or Meg), no, I don't love you. Cut to fallout. Armageddon.

Love was a mystery all right. He'd cobbled together the required love story for his grant submission and posted it with a fatalistic shrug. Maybe the Lit.

Fund would pay for his trip to Broome. If not, he'd find some other way to go. There was always a way, when you wanted something badly enough. But as for Cathy, he simply couldn't see a way to act on his gut longing for her. She already had one man giving her grief. She certainly didn't need a man like the itinerant David Hillier.

* * *

Cathy watched as David turned the car around and drove away. She raised her fingers to her face, barely touching her lips where his butterfly kiss still left a faint imprint. A man didn't kiss you on the mouth unless he desired you. His kiss had been telling her something. No, not just a quick preliminary peck before the real business began. Everything that Aaron's wet mouthings had never been, it was a gesture complete in itself, a seal between them.

The evening that had started out so wrong had turned around, all thanks to him. He'd shown her a new aspect of himself — a tender, cherishing side. When he'd wrapped his arms around her she'd let herself lean into him, accepting his strength as though he would protect her from the awful pain she was remembering.

Aaron's cruel words were branded on her memory. She'd never told another living soul what he'd said, because in her heart she dreaded he might be right. Perhaps she was incapable of loving. Perhaps she would always fail at relationships, becoming a woman who lived alone, scribbling her stories and reading her romance novels, but knowing that sort of happy ending would always elude her.

David had been simply wonderful. So easily, without a lot of words or trite assurances, he'd promised her that Aaron's words were nonsense. He'd even made her laugh! Her lips twitched at the memory. A fruitcake, indeed! She no longer felt worthless and unhappy.

Surely he cared about her? But in

what way? Again her fingers touched her lips.

She didn't get it. What did he want? After that perfect moment, he'd reverted to the chatty, good-natured man he'd been at their very first meeting on the way to Bandon Grove. Talked about his books, and the research trips that took him into wild Australia for months on end. And his final words at the door — 'Sweet Cathy' — very nice, yes, but kind of . . . brotherly.

Perhaps talking about Aaron had been a turn-off. A man didn't want to know the ins and outs of a previous relationship. Every romance was a brand-new beginning, as far as the two lovers were concerned. Well, that was the hope. Inevitably, baggage did crop up, unless you were sixteen years old. David must have had a dozen girl-friends in the past. Probably glamorous women. Editors, TV presenters, inter-viewers, poets and writers, the types he would naturally meet in the course of his job. How could Cathy Carruthers, computer technician, stack up against those paragons of confidence? Not too well! He was simply a nice man who was passing through her life. They had a few things in common. Well, quite a few, if you considered the dependent relatives, the dogs, the writing interest . . .

As she climbed into bed, Cathy came to a decision. She should get on with her own book and her own life and let David attend to his. No use running to him with every little problem. He'd said he had an application submitted for funding. He must have some new novel in mind. Well, she'd contracted with herself to write a romance. The drive had faded but perhaps she'd given up too easily. She'd find a different hero — a dark-haired good-looker like David. If she chose, she could make the pages sizzle. Why not? It was only fiction after all.

5

As Christmas approached, Cathy's glimpses of hospital wards sometimes revealed patients too ill to be cheered by tinsel chains and festive messages. She admired nurses who went about their duties with a smile and a business-like acceptance of sometimes unpleasant tasks. The grateful expressions on the faces of sick people lightened an atmosphere that could have been depressing. Caring made all the difference when you were weak and dependent.

Meaning to cheer her Nan, she showed her a photo of Pixel, captured on Cathy's mobile. To her dismay, her grandmother's lips quivered. Her tone was heartbreaking as she brushed at her tears. 'Oh Cathy, you don't know how I miss her. I lie here, worrying.'

Reassurances made no difference,

and it was all Cathy could do to keep the secret of Pixel's visit that would make her grandmother's day. Nan had grudgingly accepted that she would transfer to the rehabilitation center for a month or so. The move would take place once the skeleton staff due to the Christmas break was back to normal.

Cathy passed her grandmother a pile of cards she'd collected from the letterbox. Nan had friends dating back to her school days — a list that seemed to include cousins, nieces, nephews and former neighbors, as well as the vet, family doctor, local butcher, the Guide Dog Association and a dozen charities. She smiled as she opened the envelopes one by one, reading out messages of affection and news.

Cathy was privately ashamed of her own meager posting. Her years with Aaron had affected her social life more than she'd realized. As he'd groomed her to adhere to his routines, her friends and contacts had slipped away. The move hadn't helped.

The people she knew now, apart from David, were the casual acquaintances she met in the course of her job. One or two had sent her a Christmas card, rather as her bank had done. A friendly gesture, but hardly one to set your heart fluttering in anticipation.

★　★　★

With Christmas approaching, many of the hospital beds were vacant as discharge lists had sent home all but the seriously ill or disabled. On Nan's ward the nurses' station was deserted and those on duty were going about their work almost at a run. Bells remained unanswered as the staff hurried to do the medicine rounds and attend to IVs and hourly observations.

In the far corner of Nan's room, the patient had rung three times. Finally Cathy walked over to see if she could help. An elderly woman propped on a bedside recliner beckoned anxiously.

'Get the chair, dear. It's sliding from under my leg.'

The facing chair, supporting a heavily bandaged knee, had slipped forward. Carefully Cathy moved it back, afraid she might cause pain.

'Whatever happened to you?' She stared at the black eye and bruises.

'Water on the kitchen linoleum. Went for a skid. Kneecap shattered. They've pinned it together. Now I just have to hope it mends.'

An urgent male voice called from the next bed. 'Nurse! I have to get to the toilet quickly. Can you help me?'

'I'm not a nurse. Shall I try and find someone?'

'No, love. Just lend me an arm for support. I'm not allowed to walk by myself.'

Cathy was doubtful, but the elderly man was on his feet and determined. And the bathroom was only a couple of steps away . . . She'd helped him to the toilet by the time a nurse came by. Cathy began to explain but the girl just looked grateful.

'Everyone's rostered off for the holidays. We're trying to cope but it's bedlam. So thanks.'

It seemed odd, having men and women together in the same small ward. But Nan didn't mind.

'That's Perce. He's a character. It's a long time since I had a man in my bedroom.' Her eyes suggesting mischief, she patted Cathy's hand. 'You handled that very nicely. I'd say you're a natural.'

'It's funny you should say that. I've been thinking I might make enquiries about training as a nurse.'

'It's a worthwhile career. The girls are lovely, and they're a happy lot. While you're attending to others, you forget your own problems. That's my experience.'

* * *

Day after day passed without a call from David. Cathy resisted her own urge to ring him. The routine hospital visits and a few house calls helped fill her time. At home, she diligently laid out her chapter headings and synopsis and started working through the early pages, trying to implement David's comments where he'd scribbled some suggestions on the draft. Somehow her heart wasn't in it. Soldier on, she told herself. If a seasoned writer like David had dry spells and blocks, who was she to complain? Determined not to pursue him, Cathy counted off the days until he phoned one evening as she was reading over her manuscript.

'Hi, Cathy.'

He sounded so casual! Well, two could play that game. 'David? How have you been?'

'Working away. Mainly research at the moment. The history of Broome.'

'Yes. You mentioned that.'

'Are we still on for the Christmas visits?'

'I'm available. Unless you're busy?' Why were her legs trembling so that she needed to sit down?

'No, I'm free. Everything okay?'

'Of course. Why wouldn't it be?'

'Well, you know. The ex. Last time I saw you . . . '

Last time. The kiss she would never forget. The kiss that had spoken so tenderly, with such caring and concern. The kiss that preceded his cool departure and lengthy silence.

'I'm fine.'

'Good. Um, I'm planning a run on the beach later.'

'That's nice.' There was a silence. Did he want sweet Cathy to drop everything and come running? If he wanted a sister, she wasn't applying for the job. Her feelings didn't run in that direction and she couldn't help wanting more.

'You sound, um, preoccupied?'

'Just doing a spot of research on my book.' She allowed herself a little smile.

'Okay. Well. I'll let you get on with your work then.'

'Right. We can catch up and finalize

arrangements later in the week. Bye for now.'

Her hand was shaking as she switched off the phone. His voice seemed to linger, flowing through invisible sound waves straight into her heart.

*   *   *

Christmas was a painful experience when you were alone. In every shop, on TV and featuring on magazine covers, blared persuasions to spend. Hand-made gifts, free gift-wrapping offers, lavish jewelry, even special pet hampers — that reckless shift in mood seemed to have infected everyone, as though an incentive to forget thrift had been added to the water supply.

David and Nan were Cathy's only serious contenders for a special gift. Nan's choice would be easy. Anything she could nurture or grow would be perfect. David was another matter. Cathy thought of a dozen gifts a writer

137

might appreciate — pen, computer gadget, book . . . nothing seemed quite right. Too cheap? Too lavish? Inappropriate? Setting the problem aside, she focused on the excursion for Christmas Day. It would require quite a bit of coordination. The dogs would travel best in his SUV, as they would be on the road for several hours. They would need leads, water bowls, and bedding. Cathy intended to take a morning-tea hamper to share with Nan, and a special picnic lunch for herself and David.

As she wandered the supermarket aisles, pushing her shopping cart with its few purchases, women who must be shopping to feed an army surrounded her. Some struggled with two carts to accommodate the mountain of cans and bottled drinks, hams, turkeys, imported fruits, confectionery and chocolate brands she'd never heard of.

Amidst all these couples and family groups with their running, excited children, Cathy felt like an alien. She lingered in the pet aisle, choosing treats and rawhide chews for Banquo and Pixel. Was this to be her future life? An existence where she lived alone and saw no point in setting up a Christmas tree just for herself? Christmases spent with her grandmother or at a charity lunch with others who had no family?

Her gift shopping was done. For Nan she had a bonsai tree and a calendar with appealing animals. David's present was simply in the *too-hard* basket and she'd settled for a personal organizer, the kind of practical item that a casual friend could use.

She was wrapping his gift when Pixel flew off the couch and raced along the hall. Was it David? They'd settled details for Christmas over the phone, but perhaps he wanted to see her?

At the door, she was faced by an enormous floral arrangement; the kind of formal bouquet you might see at a funeral. Arranged in a ceramic container so heavy the delivery man had trouble holding it, the flowers and foliage almost obscured his face.

'Cathy Carruthers?'

She nodded. 'I didn't order them.'

'Some admirer you must have!'

Could they possibly be from David? She couldn't imagine him sending such an ostentatious display.

'I'd better carry them in for you, ma'am.'

She led the way to the table, the man staggering behind. 'Whew! Not many deliveries like this baby. Have a nice Christmas.'

As soon as she'd locked up, she opened the small envelope tucked among the lilies, gladioli, waratah and flax. The message must have been dictated over the phone and printed by the florist. 'Happy Christmas from Aaron. I'll meet you at Mum and Dad's as usual.'

Once again she was in shock, feeling her pulse race, her mouth go dry and her stomach clench until she wondered if she might be sick. This was way more than odd. How many times during the course of their relationship had Aaron ignored what she said? She could see his blank expression even now, as though her words simply did not compute with him. With intellectual puzzles or computer design, he was so clever.

Financially he'd established such a good life. It was always the little things, the seemingly trivial issues, which were too hard for him to grasp. He would buy her anything she wanted, but had no idea how to sit and listen quietly when she needed to talk.

He really believed she was planning to turn up in Melbourne in a few days. And then what? Pick up as though nothing had happened? Was she to spend the rest of her life moving interstate, starting again, trying to elude him? He knew her phone number. He'd found her address. Oh yes, he was smart enough to bypass privacy laws and filters.

There was only one thing to do. Cathy had his parents' contact details in her old address book. Her stomach knotted as she dialed the Melbourne number.

Half an hour later, she sat nursing a cup of tea, her hands cupped around it as though she needed to warm herself right through. Aaron's mother had been completely frank.

'I always hoped things would work out with you and Aaron,' she'd said. 'But I wasn't surprised when he told me you'd gone. Aaron has Asperger's syndrome. Do you know what that is?'

Cathy didn't. His mother explained. 'It's related to autism. Often the sufferer is highly intelligent, but the brain functions in a way that makes it very hard to process emotions and relationships.'

'Why didn't he tell me?'

'Perhaps he thought it wasn't important. Or perhaps he was afraid.'

She was forming a picture of how Aaron's condition had ruled the lives of his family. So much was suddenly making sense.

'Would that explain the routines?'

His mother sighed. 'Oh yes. The routines. We lived with them ever since he was a little boy. He couldn't tolerate changes of any kind. If I put the milk on his porridge before the sugar, he wouldn't eat it.'

'And that's why he's pursuing me now?'

'Oh yes. He has built you into his life and the fact you're gone doesn't compute. It will in time. Of course we'll talk to him and reinforce that he must leave you alone.'

There were tears in Cathy's eyes as she put the phone down. How unfair! Poor Aaron, everything decided by an unasked-for affliction. She'd judged his behavior as self-centered and cold. And so it was, but there were reasons she'd had no knowledge of.

What had caused her fear of Aaron was the lack of truth between them. Perhaps if he'd been honest . . . Instead, he'd resorted to blame and criticism until she was robbed of her femininity — a failure.

How did she feel now? She ought to have realized there was something medically wrong with Aaron. No, that was the old Cathy, blaming herself. She wasn't the one at fault. He'd been secretive. Because of Aaron's put-downs and possessiveness, she'd lost contact with friends, kept her opinions to herself, even dressed in those mousy styles he'd preferred her to wear in public. She'd been trying to rebuild her confidence. She'd bought a few new outfits he'd never have let her wear, though so far they hung unworn in the wardrobe.

All this was going to take a while to process. She looked at the flowers. How typical, to think the most showy and expensive must be the best. She'd thought more of David's single fran-gipani floret, and his whispered 'beautiful'. But her impulse to hurl the arrangement into the backyard had passed. No, why waste it? There were plenty of people in the hospital who would appreciate a few fresh flowers at Christmas. She felt drained of anger and her fear had gone. At last she understood.

Tomorrow she'd get on the internet and research Asperger's. And she would talk to David. But not tonight. A wave of exhaustion washed her into bed, where she fell into a deep sleep.

* * *

David was just back from his morning run with Banquo when the phone rang. 'Cathy! You're an early bird!'

'I want to ask you to lunch. Are you free?' She sounded different. Confident. He couldn't explain it. More open. Her guard dropped. Something.

'Lunch? Why not? Where?'

'Just at my place. It won't be fancy, but we have to finalize the visits, and I have something to tell you.'

'I have some news for you, too.'

He'd been asked to step in and act as keynote speaker at a literary luncheon in Sydney when the booked writer had bailed out. The fee was attractive, there would be sales on the day, and the media reporting would please his publisher. Quite frankly, he'd prefer lunch with Cathy any day. But it was money. The reality of life was rarely the way you imagined.

When Cathy opened her door, he did a double take. Her slim-fitting skirt ended mid-thigh, showing an extraordinary length of shapely leg. Her low-cut tank top plunged towards a deeply inviting cleavage. She wore makeup, just a little silvery eye shadow that added sparkle to her eyes, and a touch of that shiny gloss stuff that made her lips look soft and inviting. Best of all, she offered him a genuine smile of welcome.

'Where's Banquo?'

'He was asleep when I left.'

Pixel was very quiet, as though accepting him now as a member of the household.

Cathy walked ahead down the long

hall, and he had the perfect opportunity to size her up. Lunch with this gorgeous woman! Why had she been hiding her assets underneath those cover-up jeans and tops? She was a rival for any glamor girl he'd dated.

The table was set with a simple blue checked cloth, white plates, a couple of glasses. The centerpiece was a tiny sprig of rosemary in a minute vase; about as unlike that monstrous bunch of flowers on the desk as one could imagine.

'So what's been happening with you?' He waved to the arrangement, and had an awful premonition the flowers were from a new suitor. As the story unfolded, he nodded. 'As a matter of fact, one of my dad's colleagues suffered the same thing. He was a professor. Some form of genetic research to do with twins, I think it was. Interesting man.' He shook his head as Cathy opened the white wine and poised the bottle over his glass. 'Better stick to juice. I'm driving. Yes, this guy used to come to dinner with the family.

Once a month. It always had to be the first Friday of the month; nothing else would do. He could be inappropriate at times. At Mum's funeral, he suddenly went up and started telling jokes about her cooking. Embarrassing.'

'I was reading about Asperger's on the internet.' Cathy sipped her drink. 'Seems a lot of famous people are thought to have had it. Alfred Hitchcock, Mozart . . . '

'Oh yes. Einstein, Darwin, and don't forget the writers. George Orwell. Jane Austen.'

'All genius types. And Aaron certainly wasn't short of brains.' She looked reflective. 'But, David, can you imagine how you would feel if a lover sat you down with a spreadsheet and explained that in the area of relationship she had earned nine ticks, while you had eight crosses?' She leaned towards him, increasing his view of her soft, inviting cleavage.

'Oh Cathy!'

'What about this? He bought this

academic tome. *Analyzing Love*, I think it was called. He lectured me for an hour on the sub-headings. What were they — ? Judgments and aims required by love. Grounds for thinking it present. That sort of language.'

He hardly knew whether to laugh or be angry, that anyone would dare make such presumptions. For the memory had brought back the old closed look to her face. Even her posture drooped.

'The worst time was when he said I was incapable of loving.' Tears flushed her blue eyes.

He'd heard that from her before. Clearly it had cut deep into Cathy's psyche. He took her glass and gently set it down. He pulled her to her feet and hugged her, bringing their bodies into contact that was silent and spoke volumes of concern.

'Miss Carruthers, say after me: 'I am a loving person'.'

She gave an embarrassed wriggle.

'Come on! Say it.'

Very softly, she repeated the words.

'Good! Now repeat after me: 'I am beautiful, kind, loving, and absolutely gorgeous'.'

She burst out laughing. 'I can't say that, David!'

'Then I will say it for you. Cathy Carruthers, you are a beautiful, kind, loving and utterly ravishing woman, and will you do me the honor of kissing me?'

As she gave a demure nod, he found her parting lips, and felt her yield. She leaned, all softness, into him. His fingers combed through the rich waves of her hair, gently pulling her head back to receive his deepening kiss.

Over lunch, they settled details for Christmas Day. When Cathy said she planned to donate the flowers to the wards, he nodded. That was so like her, to think of others. He helped dismantle the arrangement and make several smaller bundles, and carried them out to his car. Parking at the hospital was always difficult. It would save Cathy a long, heavily burdened walk if he met her at the drop-off bay beside the main doors.

'You don't have to do this,' she protested.

'I want to. It's not far out of my way.'

It wasn't an effort to lend a hand. Sweet Cathy had shown him another dimension of her nature. She was desirable, sexy; already he didn't want to walk away.

★ ★ ★

On Christmas Day she was up early, heading to Nan's house to feed the cats and chickens before the main day started. All the ingredients for the picnic were stowed in the fridge — ham and turkey, crisp French bread, salads, mixed nuts, mince pies, a non-alcoholic wine. She'd bought a fruitcake and made a big thermos of tea to share with Nan.

Loading Pixel's gear, her picnic basket, and the presents, she locked up and drove to David's. They planned to arrive at the hospital by nine a.m. and spend an hour or so with Nan before setting out for Magnolia Gardens, Gregory's care home in Sydney. The day seemed undecided, with fitful sunshine and blue sky yielding to scudding clouds. A good day for a drive; the animals would travel more comfortably in this weather. The news report was predicting a heat wave for Perth and Broome, in Western Australia. David could look forward to those conditions for his research trip. He hadn't mentioned it lately, but she'd glimpsed his funding submission while working on his computer, and knew he intended to go west. It was a prospect she didn't want to think about. Sometimes the vastness of the continent amazed her. What stopped her from seeing the country herself? Well, finances, at present. And of course, Nan. But all that could be reviewed, one day. Since resolving the mystery of Aaron, she felt more open to life.

* * *

David was waiting and ready. He'd already fitted the dog barrier and Banquo was aboard. After sharing a friendly greeting hug, Cathy and David packed the rest of the gear, working together like a family on a day trip with the children. Keeping to their schedule, they were at the hospital as planned. The dogs, welcoming an outing, tugged on their leads while Cathy carried the smaller picnic hamper.

'I'll borrow a wheelchair and bring Nan down to that courtyard.' She pointed to an open area just outside the main doors. 'You can be waiting with the dogs. And have your mobile ready. I have to have a photo of the reunion.'

Rules on the ward were relaxed today. A number of patients were going home for a family lunch, and nobody took any notice as Cathy found a spare wheelchair in the corridor. Her grandmother beamed at her when she walked in. Nan was up and dressed. She was using crutches now for short walks, though she said they hurt her arms. She needed no persuasion to climb aboard.

Cathy would always treasure the photo that captured Nan's and Pixel's reunion.

David was waiting as arranged. Banquo was in an obedient down-stay and Pixel stood restrained by her leash. As Nan came into view, the little dog registered the appearance of her mistress. Immediately standing on her two back legs, she began to prance and pirouette, a whirling dervish in a dance of ecstasy. Nan stared, held out her arms, and called.

Pixel raced to the wheelchair and hurtled onto Nan's knee, her tiny pink tongue covering the veined hands with moist kisses that would put any lover to shame. Tears ran down Nan's cheeks. 'Pixel, Pixel. My little girl!' She looked up at Cathy. 'The best present in the world.'

David quietly released Banquo and

was introduced to Cathy's grandmother. The little group settled by an outdoor seat and spent the next hour negotiating cups of tea, cake and conversation. Nan's sharp glance was assessing the man who appeared to be sweet on her granddaughter. She listened intently as he explained about his father.

'Poor man! I feel for him. I'm only stuck here for a short while. Is he really not capable of living at home?'

'In most ways, yes. He has a little vision, just enough to make his way around. It's the fine details he can't manage, such as reading, writing, and of course monitoring his diabetes.'

'Why doesn't he pay a nurse then? Is he hard up?'

Her direct questions did not bother David, who smiled. 'No. Not exactly. He's quite well-off. But he can't live alone. He went to pieces when Mum passed away. No idea of cooking. Loneliness. You know.'

'I do.' Nan clutched Pixel firmly to

her. 'I have my animals. But an empty house can be depressing, and for a man . . . ' Her unfinished sentence suggested the male sex was hopeless at domestic detail. Seeing David's amused expression, she added: 'Oh, not you young ones! I suppose you can cook all kinds of foreign fancy-dancy dishes?'

David nodded and smiled at her — one of the dazzlers that melted any woman's resistance.

Nan just laughed out loud. 'So you're a charmer! Nothing wrong with that, but you remember, Cathy's one in a million. Just in case you haven't noticed.'

'I've noticed.'

'Hmm. Good fellow.' She was patting Banquo. 'Your father's dog? Terrible. They must miss each other. Life's unkind at times. Still, I'm a believer in happy endings. Cathy, top up my cup, dear. And I'll try another little piece of cake.'

As Cathy pushed the chair back to the ward, Nan's voice carried back to her: 'He's a deep one. A good-looker, too. Why doesn't he have his father to live with him?'

'He can't. He writes novels. The settings are rugged — West Australia, the outback. Iron and diamond mining country, that sort of thing. He travels a lot.'

'So he stays in these places? Lives there?'

'For a time, yes.'

Nan's unspoken judgment made Cathy come to his defense. 'He's not indifferent, Nan. He's taken Banquo. I think he's really worried about his dad. But he has to research the books. Then he comes home to write them.'

'He ran that workshop you went to? And you've known him all of a month?'

'Don't you like David?' She cared what her grandmother thought; the woman was no fool at summing up people.

'Like's nothing to do with it. He's very charming. You realize he's a gone goose over you?'

Cathy laughed. 'We're friends!'

'And the cow jumped over the moon. He's hooked, and by the look of that blush — ' She'd swiveled to inspect Cathy. ' — you're just as stuck on him. Just don't get hurt.'

'I can take care of myself.' Cathy parked the chair and put on the footbrake.

'So you told me when you were fifteen and running off the rails.'

'I'm not fifteen now, Nan. What are you doing for the rest of the day? I'm sorry we can't stay.'

'Pass me those crutches. Now you get going; that poor old man is waiting. I'll be fine. Pixel's happy; that's all I care about. The hospital's putting on a Christmas dinner menu. Drive carefully, dear. The roads will be busy. And Cathy . . . ' There was a glint in her eyes. 'Don't do anything I wouldn't do!'

★　★　★

David sat down to wait on the low brick wall that edged the courtyard. Banquo lay patiently beside him to await instructions, while Pixel stared into the distance, perhaps expecting her mistress to return soon. It was his habit to observe, storing mental notes for future writing. The individuals and groups here were marked by a sense of concern — an agenda going on underneath the happy laughter and gift-giving of a festive day. Their lives had been changed by illness and tragedy. While some were convalescent, others looked badly disabled or ill. A tattooed amputee in his twenties wheeled himself past, his expression aggressive as though the chair was his enemy. A gaunt, bald woman, thin as a stalk in her dressing gown, walked slowly by, puffing on a cigarette. Was this the price of speed, of nicotine?

He shuddered at the prospect of such a restricted life and turned his thoughts towards the challenges waiting for him in Western Australia. Soon he'd be there, under that hard blue sky where hawks circled, scanning the ground for carrion. Grueling territory, known equally for its wild beauty and its dangers. Drought was a killer, as the bone-scattered fringe of the Great Sandy Desert confirmed. A flash flood could turn a parched canyon into a torrent where an incautious man could be swept away in an instant.

The challenge excited him. What a contrast to this limited world! He had to go. But it was terrain that demanded respect. It was time to step up his training. A lazy jog along Nobby's beach wouldn't equip him to face the rugged landscapes he would encounter in Western Australia. Reading up on the geography and history of the pearl trading industry was fine, but he genuinely believed in hands-on experience.

The thought reminded him of Cathy as she'd stormed along the road at his workshop, and he smiled. She was emerging from the double doors now, waving as she walked towards him, easy grace in her movements.

He felt an unwelcome twinge of doubt. It was complicated now. There would be a painful price to pay when he went. And that price would be leaving the girl he suspected he was falling in love with.

6

Cathy leaned her head back on the headrest, enjoying the tantalizing drifts of David's spicy aftershave. Last Christmas with Aaron had been awful. Now his put-downs were behind her; David had helped her see them for what they were — pitiful projections of a confused mind. David had known the words she'd needed to hear. Sure, he was a wordsmith, but that didn't account for why he'd been so tender and understanding. He cared about her. And he wanted her. She was sure of that. A whole afternoon in his company stretched ahead. Perhaps the evening, too?

As Nan had predicted, the F3 was busy on Christmas Day. Drivers continually passed them, although David was driving at the speed limit. The dogs reacted to the journey in their individual ways, Banquo panting and shifting about to capture the best views and scents of a new environment, Pixel quite laid-back, reclining in her basket like a seasoned traveler. The route cut through drab green bush land, with turn-offs leading away to the coastal lakes and seaside settlements of the Central Coast. Near Sydney, the road crossed canyon-like drops and penetrated great rock walls bearing silent witness to an ancient landscape.

The traffic stream slowed approaching Sydney. By the time they reached the built-up outskirts, they were crawling. They weren't the only ones with the idea of visiting relatives on Christmas Day.

Gregory's care home was in the northwest of the city. By the time David covered the route with those bumper-to-bumper lanes of cars, it would be after midday. Cathy sat quietly, glad he wasn't one of those impatient drivers who kept edging past to achieve a single car length. He drove smoothly, his hands relaxed on the steering wheel.

'You're very quiet?' There was a question in his voice. She liked its timbre, with a hint of resonance.

'Daydreaming. Where were you last Christmas?'

'I'm not sure.' he thought a moment. 'Not with anyone special, I know that. Mum had died, Dad was heading for his health crisis and I'd broken up with my girlfriend.' He gave a short laugh. 'Funny how disasters seem necessary, in retrospect. They just slip into the jet stream of one's life.'

'I suppose that's true.' If she hadn't left Aaron and gone through the lonely, unsettling period that followed, she wouldn't be sitting here now, beside David.

She calculated they should arrive right at lunchtime. She was looking forward to sharing a relaxed picnic with David's father. 'If your dad's house is in Newcastle, why is he placed in Sydney?' It meant a long trip for David every week.

164

'It wasn't planned.' He braked as an old Chevy V8 whooshed past, bass speakers thumping. 'At the time, nothing else was available. Nobody knew Dad wasn't following his diet or attending to his medications.'

'Your mother must have acted as his eyes.'

'Yes, she did, at home. He was dependent on her. She organized everything that kept him going.'

'Poor man.' She was comparing his dark world to Nan's which was so packed with her animals, the house and garden, and her many friends. 'No wonder he went to pieces. He just collapsed one day?'

'Exactly. Luckily a neighbor found him. Banquo raised the alarm. Dad was in the hospital while they stabilized his diabetes and diagnosed clinical depression. Obviously he couldn't live on his own, and all the local rest homes were full. We had to settle for Sydney.'

'Is it a nice place?'

'As nice as any prison!' He sensed

her confusion. 'Well, there are locks on the front door, for a start.'

'Why?' She hated the idea of a grown man being locked in.

'They care for dementia patients who tend to wander. It's just hard luck for the others.'

'How does he fill his days?'

She saw his hard jaw jut as though repressing a wave of regret. 'Dad's a very intelligent man. He was a scientist. Liked nothing better than an in-depth discussion with a colleague. He likes classical music. Walking with Banquo. Life's lonely for him now.'

'Why can't he have Banquo at the home?'

'Regulations. Red tape. The place was privatized just after I got Dad settled. Animals weren't on the agenda. The library they'd advertised was a miserable shelf of reject novels. *Cowboy Jake and the Tattooed Lady*, style of thing. Not that Dad can read small print.'

'But he can see a little?'

'Oh yes. He'll be able to see you.' There was a pause as David concentrated on changing lanes. The turnoff was coming up. 'That's if you're standing fairly close. It's all the life skills that he can't handle. Small print. Street signs. Directions. Instructions. It's too easy to make mistakes when you're guessing those sorts of things.'

'Do you think he's resigned to staying where he is?'

'No.' He'd spoken abruptly, and said no more. The terse reply apparently concealed a dilemma he had no idea how to resolve. Cathy did not push him further. Within a few minutes they were pulling into the parking bay of the nursing home.

The entrance to Magnolia Gardens was impressive. Emerald lawns and colorful flowerbeds set off the old trees that had given the home its name. They were magnificent specimens, their great branches and leathery foliage outlined against the fluorescent glare of the overcast white sky. The gracious building must once have been a well-to-do family residence. Cathy could see David had tried to choose a home-like setting for his father. But, as he said, the front doors were operated by push-button locks. As David punched in the code, then tried a second time, a receptionist walked over and signaled through the glass panel.

'The numbers have been changed,' she explained, releasing the lock. 'Some of these old ones are wily. Are you coming in?'

'We'll just fetch the dogs,' David said.

'Dogs? We don't allow animals here. I'm sorry. There's a risk of cross-infection.'

'We're traveling with my father's guide dog. He has right of passage. And the small dog is a companion animal, also exempt from your rules.' He smiled at the woman, one of his real winners, but she was immune to his charm.

'I don't make the rules here. I just

administer our policies. Who are you here to see?'

'Gregory Hillier.' David controlled his emotions well, but Cathy could tell he was rapidly losing his cool.

'Why don't I fetch him out? He can sit in the gardens with you and the animals.'

'I might just 'fetch him out' myself. Excuse me.' Tugging Cathy along with him, he stepped into the foyer. 'I know the way.'

Sensing she was dismissed, the stern woman returned to the front desk.

'Another new one,' murmured David. 'They seem to change the staff here every few weeks.'

He wasn't happy at all, striding ahead past a day room where a row of elderly people sat staring into space. As they passed the door, Cathy heard a male aide shout at one woman.

'Hurry up, Martha! We don't want to mess our pants.'

At the end of a dark passage they came to a door labeled *Gregory Hillier*.

David knocked. 'Hi, Dad! Happy Christmas. This is Cathy.' He beckoned her forward, so that she was standing a few feet from a silver-haired man with a trace of David's face in his firm jaw and well-proportioned features. The cleft in his chin was the same as his son's. He stood up — a tall, still-handsome figure.

'I'm delighted to meet you, Cathy. An unexpected Christmas present. I must say I was at a loss as to how to pass my day.'

He was offering his hand in a courteous gesture. Cathy stepped into his range of vision. 'We've brought a picnic, Mr. Hillier. Will you share it?'

'Please call me Gregory. An old-fashioned appellation, I know. From the Latin, Gregorius, meaning 'watcher'. Rather ironic, wouldn't you say, given my eyesight?' He chuckled. 'Thank you for your invitation to lunch, Cathy. I do believe I shall accept. I'm not altogether overwhelmed with other offers today.'

He took his cane, and the three

returned along the passage. As they passed the day room, an attendant called out to Gregory. 'We're having a lovely singsong around the player piano later, Mr. Hillier. Don't forget.'

'My, my, what a treat.' His irony was lost on the girl, who went back to her charges.

They were duly freed from the locked foyer and walked across to the shady corner where David had left the car.

'Surprise, Dad!' He released the back door and Banquo jumped out. For a second he sniffed the air, recognizing his master's scent. Then, with a whimper of pure joy, he paced forward, lay down and rested his head on Gregory's shoes.

'So. It's you, old friend.' There was a catch in Gregory's voice as he stooped and gently pulled the dog's soft ears. There was something so moving about this dignified reunion that Cathy felt her own eyes blur with tears. Even David was biting his lower lip, trying to contain his emotions. Feeling intrusive,

Cathy busied herself with Pixel, who soon created a light-hearted mood, delighting Gregory as he peered closer and stroked her cat-like black and white fur.

It was like any happy outing in a park. The picnic rug was spread under the trees. Food and drink, the hopeful dogs, conversation, other visitors strolling with their relatives — at times it was hard to pick who, at the end of the day, would go home and who would return to the locked building.

Whatever condition Gregory had sunk to when he was admitted, he'd clearly returned to a normal state of mind now. An erudite man with a dry sense of humor, he entertained Cathy with amusing anecdotes from the past that gave her an insight into David as a little boy — the play he'd written and staged when he was seven, the time his parents found him preparing to rappel from the roof . . . Even then his mature interests had been developing.

Gregory turned to his son. 'Was your

mother alive last Christmas? Or was it the year before? One loses track of time in here.'

'It was the year before, Dad. You stayed on by yourself at home for nine months, and you've been here since May.'

'That long? I'm not surprised. It feels like seven years, not seven months. So when do I go home, David?'

It was the one question his son did not want to answer.

'Dad, that's not going to happen.'

'What are you talking about? Of course I'm going home! I'm not a child.'

'You can't live alone. You can't cook; you can't handle your medications. You'll have another diabetic crisis.'

'That's no problem.' Gregory produced a letter from his shirt pocket. 'Glory wants to stay with me. She can do all that.'

David's expression was a mask of disbelief. 'Glory! You've got to be joking!'

Cathy was listening to this exchange. David saw she had no idea what they were talking about.

'Dad's referring to his sister. She spends her life on cruise ships, going around the world. She's the maddest woman I've ever met, even if she is my aunt.'

'Glory's not mad, David. Eccentric. Unpredictable. Not mad.'

'Okay. Eccentric. Unpredictable. Totally unreliable. She couldn't care for an axolotl, much less you, Dad.'

'Well, here's what she says. She's getting off the boat next month, and she wants to take a break from cruising until June. She wants to come and stay with me. At home.'

'And after June?' David was shaking his head as he stood up. 'I think I'll go for a walk.'

As he strode away, Gregory turned to Cathy with a wink. 'That boy always walks away when things get difficult. Don't you put up with it, Cathy. Fond of him, are you?' They sat close enough that he could see her blush. 'Thought so.' He was patting Banquo, who lay panting quietly at his side. 'Life's not much without love. My wife and I had forty-one happy years. She's gone now, and they plan to keep me here, like a dusty old suit hanging in the wardrobe. I'm not having it. I'm not spending the rest of my days listening to 'Jingle Bells' on the player piano. If Glory's prepared to look after me, she'll do.'

Cathy had to admire his spirit. Yet she could understand David. If his aunt was really so unreliable, Gregory would be left at home alone, and the whole problem would fall back on his son's shoulders.

The topic was dropped when David returned. Gregory and Banquo set off together for their own private outing. Cathy finished packing up the remains of the picnic. David lay back on the rug, staring through the branches to the patchy, clouded sky.

'It's a difficult situation,' Cathy suggested, wanting to support him, but he just shook his head in an irritable way.

'I don't want to talk about it,' was all he said.

She left him there and set off with Pixel, whose friendly mannerisms delighted everyone she passed. As she bounded past a wheelchair, its confused occupant called after her: 'Buster, come back, you naughty boy! Come here to me at once!'

And Cathy thought how everybody confined here had once had a home, a family, pets, and an independent life. No wonder Gregory couldn't accept this life. Like David, he was stubborn. He wouldn't give in without a fight.

By mutual consent, the men's disagreement had been dropped. David talked about his next novel and the luncheon he was to address. Gregory seemed to know quite a bit about the history of the pearling industry, even as far back as aboriginal trading in pearl shell. Watching the two men chat and joke together, Cathy felt envious. She'd never known that bond. Just a toddler when her father had died in a car accident, she'd disliked her strict stepfather on sight, and the relationship had only grown worse as she reached puberty. Her one regret when she heard he'd migrated back to Germany was that her mother went with him, leaving her effectively an orphan. Without Nan, Cathy might have become one of society's misfits. No wonder she felt she would do anything for her grand-mother.

As the afternoon wore on, the male aide left the building and walked over to them. 'You'd better get inside unless you want to miss your dinner,' he said to Gregory, who sighed and levered himself upright.

'But it's only four o'clock,' Cathy protested as Gregory laid a placating hand on her arm.

'Doesn't pay to complain.' He spoke lightly, but she wondered what he meant.

Caressing Banquo, he walked away,

not turning to wave as he was shepherded through the entrance door. Unspoken emotion lay heavy in the air as David loaded the dogs and Cathy cleared away the remains of the picnic.

David was quiet on the drive home. His hands gripped the wheel, his mouth tightening at times as though he was replaying the unresolved conversation with Gregory. Topics Cathy broached seemed to drift away after a few terse words. She fell silent, letting the soft thrumming of the road noise lull her into reverie. She was happy, even if David wasn't. She'd talk to him when he was in a better frame of mind; try to convince him that his father had a right to follow his wishes, even if they failed. At worst, he would see he was attempting the impossible. But perhaps his dad's sister wasn't as bad as David remembered.

'Where are we going?' The car had turned off the freeway.

'Pit stop. I could use a leg stretch. How about you?'

She nodded. The dogs would like to get out of their cramped quarters. David stopped by a grassy park on the shores of Lake Munmorah. Most of the day-trippers had gone by now. The only signs of life were a few lone fishermen casting from the bridge, and a pelican colony strutting at the water's edge. Cathy kept Pixel on a leash; the birds were three times her size and she'd once read of a Chihuahua being picked up and carried off by a pelican.

She checked the picnic basket. 'The tea's finished. Want a cold drink?'

They shared the last can of Sprite and one crumbling mince pie. Here, on the edge of the lake, they were far from every worldly problem. Nan's accident, Aaron's illness, Gregory's confinement . . . nothing could be done about them now. Soon it would be evening.

'It was a good day.' She took his hand. 'Thank you.'

He smiled at her. 'Happy Christmas, Cathy.'

As he leaned across and kissed her,

she knew this Christmas would stay in her memory. One of the best days. A day for David and Cathy and the two weary dogs waiting for their dinner.

* * *

'Are you coming in?'

Cathy hesitated. He sounded as though he didn't mind one way or the other. But she'd been close to him all day, often only a few inches away from that electric charge that shocked her into goose bumps. And she hadn't given him his gift. In the haste of the morning's departure she'd left it behind. Now she had another dilemma. If he had nothing for her, wouldn't it embarrass them both if she pulled it out? Fortunately he spoke.

'I'm an idiot! I haven't given you your Christmas present. We'll have a scratch meal if you're hungry.'

'Pixel needs feeding, David.'

Now he was persuasive. 'Cold chicken? Salami? Would that suit madam?'

180

Cathy laughed. 'I'm sure she'll approve.'

The dogs were given a quick walk and their supper, then both collapsed on Banquo's mattress.

'That's the kids seen to.' Now he was home, David sounded light-hearted. 'Now. Your turn.'

They each produced gift-wrapped packages, strangely alike. As the paper fell away, they burst into laughter. The two organizers were identical, down to the leather covers, calculators and stainless steel pens.

'Great minds . . . '

All day they'd picnicked and nibbled, and neither felt hungry now. Cathy accepted the offer of coffee and crackers with assorted cheeses. Afterwards, a wave of fatigue flowed through her limbs. She'd been on the go since early morning and, as well as the distance they'd covered, she'd found the day emotional. Her gaze met David's. He was leaning back on a black beanbag, long legs stretched out, hands clasped behind his head, the picture of relaxation. She was reminded of a lithe, powerful animal, a panther perhaps, totally in command of his den. He looked irresistible. She thought if he summoned her she would go to him, drawn by his magnetism as he simply sat motionless, watching her.

'Sleepy?' was all he said.

She nodded. There was no need to recap the day's events. She had no urge to busy herself, collect Pixel or drive home to the empty house.

'Mmm.' He apparently felt the same. Yet it wasn't that kind of weariness that makes a soft bed so inviting. An utter peacefulness filled the room: two spirits in accord, no need of conversation; a time simply to be there, together.

'Come over here?' He patted the beanbag, which was the size of a small sofa, and she went and settled beside him. The soft packing nestled around her hips, molding her against his body. Her head leaned onto his shoulder. By glancing up she could see the planes and angles of his facial bones, the firm jaw with its cleft like his father's, the sculptured nose and cheekbones. His black hair was wild and his black fitted T-shirt clung tightly to his athletic shoulders and toned chest.

'Comfy?'

The heat of his body blended with hers. Cathy stretched languidly, cat-like, deliberately pressing the length of her leg against his. She reached up, her fingers combing through his hair. His arm eased around her shoulders. They shifted together, sinking deeper into the beanbag, hips touching. She eased onto her side a little, making him aware of her cleavage, drawing his gaze to focus there. A spasm of desire cramped her womb as gently he slid his hand into the opening of her blouse and toyed with her plump flesh, straying into her bra until he found her nipple. As it firmed, a stronger spasm made her shiver.

David shifted again, more deliberately, so she could feel his erection.

Assuming a superior angle, he was gazing at her intently as though memorizing her features.

'You are so beautiful,' he murmured, his voice low and ragged.

She did not reply, just moved a little, pressing against him, making him know he was desired.

The peaceful mood had changed and the focus in the room was their bodies, clamped hard together as though seeking some secret entrance to the other. His mouth covered hers, their languid tongues winding and thrusting and sliding in a ritual of pleasure. She felt desirable, unresisting. She was offering herself to him. He could take her. Gently. Urgently. Passionately. However he came to her, her body would welcome him and tell him he was home.

They eased out of the kiss and Cathy's head was tilted back, her pale throat bared to him. Her tangled caramel-blonde hair flared loosely; her glass-bright sapphire eyes gazed up at him. Her flushed face and swollen lips told him what she wanted. He fluttered tiny kisses along that yielding throat, up and down, up and down, while she moaned softly, willing him not to stop. Momentary thoughts surfaced. She hadn't showered. Did he have protection? These doubts ebbed away just as quickly as they arose.

They were both breathing heavily. Now their movements were rough, impatient. He watched her drag off her top and bra, while he wrenched off his shirt and threw it on the floor. He tugged at her zipper and eased off her skirt. They lay bare breast to breast, the heat of the night bringing a faint slippery sheen to their clinging skin. David's fingers moved along her spine, sought low down on her back, finding the sensitive nerve plexus and teasing it, circling round and round until she quivered with sensation. Retaliating, she pinched his dark nipples, then her own. She felt wanton, ready for anything he wanted. Panting, she reached down to his jeans.

And he pulled away. As though shocked from a deep dream, she felt utterly confused. She was on the point of surrender. What was he doing? He sat up, gasping, his profile harsh, distorted with self-control.

'Cathy? Are you sure we should do this?'

'What?' She was bewildered, her eyes unfocused. She did not know or care what he wanted to say, and reached for his arm, trying to pull him back into the dream.

'Are you on the pill, or something?'

Reality was seeping through. Cold, hard, horrible reality. No, she wasn't on the pill. Or something. She had been, all those years with Aaron. She'd been celibate for months, and had decided to give her body a rest from chemicals.

'Don't you have anything?' Her voice sounded pitiful, dismayed.

'No call for it lately. Sorry.' He was abrupt, still coming down from the point so close to no return.

So he was celibate too. And they'd driven each other to the point of desperation, only to be deprived of fulfillment. All that was left was shakily to get dressed. She felt a fool. Apparently he did too. They'd behaved like teenagers, driven by desire and to hang with the consequences. Almost. He'd been the one to remember. Cathy hardly needed to add to her list of problems an unplanned pregnancy. Probably she should thank him, but at the moment she wasn't grateful. They could not think of much to say. He offered her a cup of tea. She said she didn't want one. She gathered Pixel and her new organizer and went home.

★ ★ ★

David watched the car pull away. He needed to move, not be cooped up in the stuffy apartment with a snoring dog. Striding out, he headed for the beach. The crashing of the waves built as he crossed the road and slithered down to the sand.

The whole day had been disturbing. His father's situation confronted him, without solution. The idea of Glory looking after Gregory was mad. Simply mad. It would last a few weeks, then fall apart and David would be called to pick up the pieces. Except that he would probably be on the opposite side of the continent by that time.

Then there was Cathy. There was no answer there, either. It was probably lucky they'd both been unprepared. Cathy didn't need or want a casual lover. A here-today, gone-tomorrow man was not her style. Everything she said and did spoke otherwise. She was no casual good-time girl. Once she made a commitment, whether to an old woman or a scrappy dog, she would not renege.

There were hidden depths to Cathy. He'd seen them, barely an hour ago. He'd glimpsed the passionate woman, holding nothing back — the kind of woman a man dreamed of, except that was the stuff of fantasy, of fiction. The kind of thing he'd written often enough, knowing his words had to create a scene. The kind of thing one skimmed over, accepting the scene as a minor part of a more interesting narrative.

Cathy was no minor part of his life. If he wasn't careful, he'd be in so deep his whole life would have to change. Right now he could come and go. A wife and kids would soon put paid to that. Wife? Kids? What was he thinking? He'd done perfectly well without those trappings up to now. You couldn't write his kind of books with babies crying, toddlers with chicken pox, or a pregnant wife with morning sickness.

So did he want to have an affair with Cathy? A fling and then goodbye? He'd done that, more often than he was proud of. The women ended up in tears, or angry, but it didn't matter when he was traveling and out of reach. He couldn't do that to Cathy. She was recovering from a relationship that had left a residue of hurt. He wasn't going to inflict any more pain on her.

He turned back. He didn't feel like walking, jogging, or swimming. He didn't feel like anything, except being in Cathy's bed, close to her, molded into her lovely supple curves, at rest.

The beauty of the dark night and shushing waves escaped him. Frowning, he walked home. He should have a shower, do something to relieve the engorged ache from the frustration of interrupted arousal. He couldn't be bothered. The beanbag reproached him, a lonely hollow of emptiness. He tossed down a couple of beers and went to bed.

As he drifted off to sleep, he resolved to set himself a regular work schedule. Starting tomorrow. He had his speech to prepare for the luncheon address. He should be working on the first draft of the new novel. He should definitely stay away from Cathy. You didn't put your hand in the fire when you knew what a burn felt like.

She'd found some place in him he didn't even know existed. He wanted her. Badly. But the timing was all wrong. He had commitments, plans, and they didn't include settling down nicely in Newcastle with Cathy, an aged parent and an old dog. There were hard decisions to be made.

Angry, he thumped the pillow, wanting the feel of a soft yielding touch. Cathy's touch. *Stay away from her*. He drilled the words into his resisting brain, and wondered if he had the strength to follow his own advice.

7

Nan's convalescence was proceeding well, but she did not welcome the advice of her surgeon, the physiotherapist or the social worker, who all advised she must be fully rehabilitated at the Royal Newcastle Center before she could go home.

'I can manage by myself.'

She was adamant, but Cathy only had to look at her to know the professionals were right. Bearing weight on the injured hip was out of the question until full healing had taken place. Meanwhile, crutches allowed her to hobble down the corridor or to the showers. She was determined to have afternoon tea at the cafeteria, but even that short distance was too much for her, and Cathy had to bring a wheelchair to see her back to the ward.

'You'll just have to be patient, Nan.'

The advice Cathy was giving herself was cold comfort. A full week had passed. Today was New Year's Eve and she hadn't heard a word from David since that memorable Christmas night. She wasn't going to chase him. Surely it was up to him to contact her? Unless she'd put him off. Never had she felt passion like they'd shared. Not once. With poor Aaron and a couple of earlier boyfriends it had been more like safe-crackers intent on storming the bank, rather than lovers.

Even the memory of that night brought a flush to her cheeks.

'You're looking mighty thoughtful.' Nan was settled back in her bedside chair, the hated crutches banished. 'I suppose it's that fellow.'

Of course she knew! Nan was no old lady remote from the realities of life. Cathy nodded. 'That fellow. Yes.'

'What's the problem?'

'I like him too much.'

'Meaning, you like him more than he likes you?'

Again Cathy nodded.

'And how do you know that?'

'We were together ... Now he's disappeared off the face of the earth. I think he's dumped me, Nan.'

'Together, eh?'

'I'm not a child, you know. I'm twenty-five.'

'Never said you were a child. This love business is hard at any age. People think it's all romance and bubbles, but men do go to ground when they hear the hounds baying.'

'I'm not hunting him!'

'That's what you say. He's the elusive type. I picked that up right away. How old is the man? Thirties? Never been married, you told me. Comes and goes as he pleases. And then you show up. I saw the way he looked at you. I told you.'

'Yes. A gone goose. I remember!'

'He's scared, Cathy. I'll bet a box of matches he's moping around, his fingers itching to give you a call.'

'Do you think so?' Oh, how she

wanted to believe Nan's words.

'Why don't you ring him yourself?'

'I've thought about it . . . ' Thought about it, planned it, held a dozen different conversations with him in her mind.

'Just do it, there's a good girl. Be brave. What's the worst that can happen?'

'I guess you're right.' She dropped a kiss on Nan's cheek. 'Thanks for the advice.'

Cathy gathered her bag and stood up to leave, replacing a few of Nan's old magazines with a new pile. The horoscope she'd read dropped onto the floor. What had Virgo's annual prediction been? Something to do with a sea change, extended study, fun and romance? At least she could relate to the study part. The more time she spent at the hospital, the more she felt drawn to a career change. Already she'd looked up information on the internet. The training was a university course; another reason she felt grateful to Nan, who'd chivvied her to study and get a good result on her final exams.

As she stooped to pick up the magazine, Nan reached out and patted her head. It was a gesture Cathy remembered from her childhood; the kind of touch that was equally soothing to nervous animals and confused adolescents.

'What will be will be, dear.'

Just another of Nan's clichés, perhaps. But worrying was certainly getting Cathy nowhere. Nan was right. She ought to speak to David. At least she'd know then where she stood.

* * *

The morning staff were handing over the report to the next shift. The camaraderie among the women was obvious, and she thought how good it would be to work as part of a team, trained and prepared to take their role in the healing of their patients. In Melbourne, Cathy had worked with a group of technical staff. There she'd been able to confer and exchange ideas, but it must be so much more rewarding to work on people problems rather than machines. Her new situation emphasized that her job was solitary. She was a sole operator, and the nature of her job gave no continuity with clients. No wonder nursing appealed.

The stages of life surrounded her as she walked along the corridor. Patients were wheeled past — a baby in a cot, a young man in a wheelchair, an elderly man propelled on a gurney. There was little time for artifice here. People in crisis were stripped of pretense. Emotion creased their faces as they confronted unthinkable hurdles. Nurses worked at the front line, and already Cathy knew she was meant to be among them. She had a keen mind, and would enjoy the study. The courses offered at the university sounded wonderful. And with a Bachelor in Nursing, there were endless areas of work. A Masters qualification could lead to Practice Nursing, working side by side with doctors. The sooner she could apply, the happier she'd be. The feeling she'd found a vocation, rather than just a job, seemed a great start to the brand-new year.

Her buoyant mood drained away as she arrived home. Pixel was sound asleep, curled on Cathy's pillow. No messages on her mobile or landline. So much for auld lang syne. She'd be celebrating the New Year alone. Unless . . . Nan's advice rang in her head. What was the worst that could happen? The worst was already here.

She dialed and waited, suddenly hoping he wouldn't answer. But his resonant voice spoke into her ear, waking all the feelings she'd spent a week repressing, and she almost flung the phone away from her.

'David, it's Cathy.' She felt sick.

Well, obviously it was Cathy. He said hello. Waited.

'What's doing?' she asked.

He said he'd been working on his talk

and writing up notes for the new book. She tried and failed to visualize his face. Bored? Annoyed? Indifferent?

'I was just wondering . . . It's New Year's Eve . . . ' Pathetic. 'I suppose you're busy?'

She was giving him an out. In ten seconds this would be over. She could hang up; break down. How long could ten seconds be? Had he passed out? Worse — was some other girl with him?

'I'm not busy.' He spoke as though someone had a gun at his back. Was he that unhappy to hear from her?

'Oh. I just wondered. They're having fireworks at Nobby's Beach.'

'Mmhmm. I read that.'

'You wouldn't like to go.' It was a statement. This was the worst phone call of her life.

'What I'd like has nothing to do with it.' His spill of words reminded her of a bottle that had popped its cork. 'Yes, I would like to go to the fireworks with you. Actually, Cathy, I'd like to go anywhere with you. It's just not a good idea.'

'It isn't?' Now what was he about to produce? Secret wife? Criminal record? Terminal disease? 'Do you feel like telling me why?'

'You sure you want to know?' Five seconds. Ten. 'Okay, Cathy. Here it is. I'm falling in love with you. And I'll be leaving here soon. Does that grab you as a good prospect? I'm telling you, if you happen to be thinking of a relationship, I'm the wrong man for you. I won't be here.'

'And that's why you're avoiding me?'

'That's why I'm avoiding you.'

She felt happy. Madly, illogically happy. 'Please stop, David. Will you take me to the fireworks tonight?'

'Did you hear me? You got the message?'

'I got the message. I'll be ready at seven.'

'I'll be there. I think you're crazy.'

'Probably. Bye, David.'

She felt like dancing, or hugging

someone, or letting out a big woo-hoo! There was no one there but Pixel, who came wandering out, looking for entertainment. Cathy scooped her up and kissed her tiny black nose.

'I'm in love! David loves me. I love him. What do you think about that?'

As for his warning, she understood. *What will be will be, Cathy.* Nan was right. She couldn't control life. She could only ride this lovely wave, and hope she wouldn't get dumped.

Cathy had a long shower. She shaved her legs and underarms. She washed and conditioned her hair. She brushed her teeth, plucked her eyebrows and painted her toenails while the egg-white face mask dried. She laid out her best black bra and lacy panties. She cleaned off the mask and spent fifteen minutes applying base coat, foundation, blusher, mineral powder, mascara, eye liner and a grey-violet eye shadow ensemble to highlight her blue eyes. She tweezed a tiny hair near her nose. Her eyebrows were quite dark but she ran a light line over them anyway. She chose a lipstick to complement her red tank top and nail color. She used her blow dryer on her hair. She didn't like the result. She sprayed her hair with volumizer and did the exercise all over again. She applied Dolce and Gabbana Light Blue, her signature perfume, to every pulse spot she could think of.

She got dressed in her best Country Road jeans. Nothing formal; they were going to the beach, after all. The neckline of the red top wouldn't sit right. It seemed to be hanging to the left. She tried on the violet-blue one, decided it clashed with her red toenails, cleaned off the varnish and applied a hot pink coat instead. Now her lipstick shade was wrong. She scrubbed her lips clean and used a matching color. She changed her mind about gold earrings and spent five minutes hunting for her silver ones. The wedge sandals she'd planned to wear were looking scuffed. She took out the shoebox with her new pair, the strappy ones she'd bought on sale and thriftily stored away for next year. She put them on. She sorted out a jacket, in case the sea breeze was cool.

Cathy was ready. It was six o'clock. She gave Pixel her evening meal. Her stomach was churning. She didn't want to eat. She turned on the news and sat down to wait for David.

★ ★ ★

Why were his legs taking him to the health and beauty aisle of the super-market? Most people had finished shopping for tonight's festivities and New Year's Day. A few stragglers came and went while the bored checkout operators counted down the hours till closing time. An extremely obese woman in a motorized wheelchair signaled to David.

'Would you mind reaching down that box of tissues? No, the frangipani box.'

He waited until she'd moved on, then found what he was looking for. A man who didn't bother to carry protection deserved everything he got. Or didn't get. Not that he was planning anything. In fact, he wasn't happy with himself. The first sign of temptation and he'd buckled.

It had been an endless week. Reminders of Cathy were everywhere. His pulse went crazy at the mere ringtone of his phone. On the beach with Banquo, he thought he saw her and broke into a jog, his heart plummeting when he came close and realized the woman was a stranger. Even as he reminded himself to stay away, he grabbed his cellphone, his thumb hovering over her number before he tossed the phone aside. Cathy had suffered enough with that jerk in Melbourne. She'd been far too quick to forgive him, but that was Cathy. He didn't deserve her and he certainly wasn't going to mislead her.

As long as he'd kept busy and reminded himself of his good reasons to stay away from Cathy, he'd had the satisfaction of thinking he was showing responsibility. Just one call, her soft voice, his memories of Christmas night . . . And here he was, a robot driven by his lustful nature — a nature that obediently kicked in even at the thought of her, causing him to thoughtfully peruse a stacked display of Bran Buds while he waited for his erection to subside.

Back at his apartment, he collected Banquo and set out for a good jog that would ensure the dog would sleep soundly while David was out. At home, he doubled the biscuit rations and shifted Banquo's mattress into his bedroom, which would be insulated from the noise of the fireworks.

He was hungry. There was leftover curry, but that tended to leave one with a strong body odor. He heated a frozen pizza and ate the lot, then took a shower, used deodorant and cologne, and shaved twice. He put on fresh clothes. It was six o'clock. He turned on the news and slumped in the beanbag until it was time to collect Cathy.

* * *

Parking at the beach would be next to impossible. Already, rowdy groups of revelers were weaving down the middle of the road, waving and shouting out as vehicles slowed and tooted.

'I'll park at Honeysuckle. We can walk from here.'

Locking the car securely, David linked arms with Cathy and they set out along the foreshore. She felt dizzy with happiness. They had come so close to parting. She'd been so sure David had withdrawn and was already looking ahead to his next book, his trip, another casual liaison. To be walking in step like this, knowing what he'd admitted, seemed like an impossible answer to her dreams. The evening was infused with magic as she gazed around an area she hadn't visited since girlhood.

During the past five years while she'd

been in Melbourne, the waterfront had undergone major reconstruction. Multi-story apartments had sprung up along the stretch where previously, industrial sheds had lined the wharves. Ships still queued out to sea, awaiting their turn to berth at Newcastle, one of the biggest exporters of coal in the world. Three-hundred-meter freight carriers were shepherded into the port by tiny tugs, and at night the harbor glittered with the lights of ferries, fishing boats and private vessels. The vibrant picture was enhanced by happy crowds preparing to see in the New Year. It was still too early for the nightclubs to be swinging, but restaurants were packed with diners booked for a luxury meal.

'Would you like to stop for a drink?'

She nodded and felt her heart skip with happiness. Here they were: a couple, like all the other couples making their way towards the beach at the far end of the promenade.

'I'd love a cocktail.' It was a night to go for broke. David ordered her favorite

Sunset Tequila and a light beer for himself. The crowd was noisy; one had to shout, and it seemed easier simply to sit facing each other, their eyes conversing silently.

They left the bar and wandered on, coming to Nobby's Beach where families had staked out camp spots with picnic rugs, food and drink. Frisbees and kites soared above the racing children. Surfers rode the small swell while the sky flared and dwindled, promising a perfect showcase for the coming fireworks display.

'Will Banquo be okay by himself?'

'He's securely shut up, and I left the TV going to drown out any noise.'

'I did the same.' Pixel was slightly deaf, and didn't care even when thunder had Cathy cowering in her bed. Strange, she'd never before had this constant awareness of another's needs. David must be experiencing the same thing with the guide dog. She smiled to herself, thinking that perhaps they were both getting into practice for a day in the future when they might have children. But that was one thought she had no intention of sharing with him tonight.

Finding a space, they spread the rug and sat close, enjoying the convivial mood. Just for tonight, nobody cared about global debt, natural disasters or the endless outpouring of gloomy news from the media. The dawn of a brand-new year brought hope reflected on the smiling faces, the happy music of local bands, and the mouth-watering aromas of food sizzling on portable barbecues.

As the display was intended for families, the pyrotechnics began at nine p.m. The navy-blue sky bloomed with crimson, emerald and silver bursts of light. Rockets streaked skyward, their torpedo trails exploding in golden showers. Cannon crackers shook the ground, while pinwheels spun madly and disintegrated, dropping bright blue sparklers.

The display lasted for fifteen minutes

before the last few squibs popped and faded, leaving only the breaking of waves beneath a quiet sky. Most people started to gather their children and goods, preparing to head home.

Cathy settled back in the crook of David's arm. She felt small and safe, a single sentient cell amid the vast spaciousness of sky and ocean. Here there was no past or future, no place for worry or doubt. They were together.

He pulled her closer. 'I've missed you.'

She nodded. 'Me too. It was awful.'

'It's just . . . '

She hushed him. 'Don't talk. Just hold me like this.'

*   *   *

He dropped a soft kiss on her eager lips and settled against her, pulling her close. She felt there was no goal, no hurry. Desire could wait. A sense of belonging flowed between them and the problems of the future drifted away.

* * *

A breeze stirred the coarse dune grass. At the end of the breakwall, the lighthouse blinked. A solitary gull mewed, as by mutual consent they sat up, stretching. Cathy gave a shiver and pulled on her jacket.

'Ready to walk back?'

'Yes.'

Their steps in harmony, arms around each other, they followed the return path to the car. David parked outside her house.

'Are you coming in?' she asked.

'You sure?'

Illuminated by the street light, her smile was radiant. 'Quite.' She spoke again, after a pause. 'Did you remember — ?'

Now it was David who grinned, patting his pocket. 'I did.'

Pixel, quite unconcerned about the fireworks, greeted them, inspected the visitor and departed to go back to sleep on the end of Cathy's bed.

Quietly, David and Cathy embraced, their hands caressing, their bodies melding together. He led her along the passage to her bedroom. Without hurry, he helped pull off her top, her jeans, the special undies. With a gaze of reverence he stood absorbing the slender loveliness of her naked form. Cathy watched as he stripped, uncovering his masculine physique.

As though approaching a sacred ritual, a ceremony after which they would be forever changed, they lay together on the bed, refreshing their senses, kissing, making slow and tender love. Once, Pixel lifted her head, stared at them for a moment, and with a contented sigh went back to sleep.

* * *

With nothing formalized in words, they were a couple now. Much of life was the same. The holiday period was over and Cathy's work picked up. Word of mouth was starting to work in her favor as satisfied clients recommended her service and prices. Most days she had at least one call-out booked, and her worries over money eased enough to take advantage of the post-Christmas sales. Clothing stores were lining up the autumn fashions, and summer wear was going for a song. Feeling feminine and desirable, she bought several new outfits: pretty, floaty styles in vibrant shades that seemed to match her off-the-ground mood of elation.

Nan had been moved to the rehabilitation center next to John Hunter Hospital. Cathy kept up regular visits but was relieved to sense her grandmother did not feel quite so restricted now. In fact the staff encouraged her to move about as much as possible, building up her strength to cope with the strain of using crutches. She was scheduled to use the warm pool as soon as her doctor gave the all-clear to weight-bear on her hip repair. The regular chair exercise classes seemed to please her. Wearing a Lycra top and with her hair held back by a headband, she looked like a candidate for the senior Olympics.

She showed a keen interest in the progress of Cathy's love life. 'So where's he taking you tonight?' Nan was remembering her own courting days and the dance band that played in the old church hall. She liked hearing about their walks on the beach, shared meals, and the DVDs they rented and watched, curled together in his bean-bag. But the news that David was soon going to Sydney for a week drew her disapproval. Her reaction to his literary luncheon talk made Cathy laugh.

'Watch him! There'll be plenty of women there making a play for him. That's why people go to those things.'

'No it's not! People are interested in current books and publishing trends.'

'What, pay eighty dollars to eat a few snacks and listen to a lot of palaver? No, those city girls will be looking for a husband with good looks and a name. What are you wearing?'

'I'm not going. The animals, remember?'

Nan was contrite. 'My cats and chickens, and Pixel.' She sounded remorseful. 'I'm so sorry, putting this load on you, dear.'

'It's not a load. I'm quite used to it now. I'll probably miss it once you're home.'

Cathy hid the doubt she felt about that outcome. While chicks hatched and pretty wild kittens had joined the pack, nobody was facing the realities of breeding. Very soon a ranger from the RSPCA would have to be called to remove the ever-growing feral population, or at least make sure the cats were neutered. Cathy loved animals but, even if Nan somehow returned home, her ever-accommodating nature would have to face facts.

The physiotherapist had said that while the hip was healing nicely, Nan's mobility would be compromised for up to a year. Daily walks would be essential, but going out alone would be unwise. If she did happen to stumble again, without a supportive arm to lean on, she might not be so lucky next time.

'You're really saying she shouldn't be by herself?' Cathy had asked.

'That's right. She won't need nursing care. In fact, the best place for her is back in her home with all her normal activities. She just needs a companion, someone to walk with her and keep an eye on things. She has no sister or cousin who might help?'

'Nobody.' Cathy shook her head. The prospect of being Nan's assistant for the rest of her life was too daunting for her to think about.

★ ★ ★

As she and David came to know each other better, she felt she was exploring a treasure house of discovery. He was such a private man. Behind the public persona resided a reserved, thoughtful man of many facets. He was no fence-sitter, venting passionate views on ecology and the global outlook. Soon she just accepted these outbursts as evidence of his deep caring. He wanted to contribute to the earth's survival, and explained that his books tried to reflect the controversies he saw when big business fuelled the human need to expand and grow rich at the planet's expense. If he asked her opinion, he considered what she said. Other men she'd known had disliked her well-meant advice, but David listened.

In the midst of some serious discussion, he could switch from thinker to outdoor man in a flash, suddenly interrupting the topic to announce he needed to go for a run or a swim. He laughed at the quirks and foibles of human nature and she was glad. She couldn't stand a man who had no sense of humor.

And David was a surprising lover. Poor Aaron must have learned his routine from some manual, and if she'd tried to initiate anything he became upset. But with David she could never predict when or where they would make love. She would look up to find his deep, hypnotic eyes boring into her blue gaze, inviting her. Each time was like a private dance, its steps never quite the same. She'd somehow believed men were really only interested in the climax of sex, that preliminaries were a duty they had to hurry through. But David liked to delay, taking as much pleasure from foreplay as she did. He found erotic points on her body that she did not even know existed. He would linger there; smiling as he heard tiny moans and gasps escaping her lips.

David's touches expressed his heart. They were sometimes gentle, sometimes rough in a careful way that made him smile down at her as she gasped with desire. Gradually she was learning the secrets of his body — the little mole on his left shoulder blade and the thin white scar on his calf, a childhood legacy after he fell out of a tree in the garden. When he slept he usually ended up on his stomach, his arms flung high on the pillow as though he was engaged in some long-distance dreamtime swim.

Absorbed in their new romance, and busy with everyday earning and duties, Cathy could hardly believe how quickly the weeks were passing. Nan would soon progress from crutches to a walker, and was using the therapy pool to exercise her weak leg muscles. David was nervous about his upcoming speech, after his publisher had told him it would be a publicity event with reporters and possibly television exposure. An interview had been lined up for him on Book World, and the luncheon in the conference room of the Hyatt Regency was sold out.

★ ★ ★

'Well?' He'd just practiced his speech for the third time, and Cathy was running out of comments. It was hard to laugh at jokes he'd already recited, and the sight of him pacing around the room, checking his notes, somehow made her nervous.

'Honestly? It's a bit detached. I mean, it sounds rehearsed.'

'Of course it does. That's what I'm doing.' He was edgy.

'Have you thought of just speaking off the cuff? I mean, when you talk to me about your books, all that conflict between sustainable development and raping the land, I feel engaged. You obviously care about your themes. I don't think you have to deliver stand-up jokes to gain audience attention.'

She expected him to flare up in anger, for he'd spent so much time refining and rewriting the talk. But he just nodded and said no more. Quietly, she boiled the kettle, made tea and set out the small iced carrot cake she'd brought from home.

'You're good for me.' He was digging in to her baking. 'Very nice.'

'It's just made from a cake mix.'

'Whatever. Full marks. I think you're right. About the talk. A written speech never comes across as sincere. I'm not a politician, so I guess I can say whatever comes into my head.'

'Wish I could be there.' She knew she had to stay and see to all the animals. The week would drag, but one big decision of her own was looming. She had received the application papers for the nursing course, reading them with growing certainty that she wanted this big shift in her life. She had time to think about it, as the current intake was full. It was just another major event in a time of change. Whatever the meaning of that prediction about a Virgo sea change, the astrologer had been right on the button there.

'Go halves on the last piece?'

'You have it. So will you really be on TV?'

'Who knows? Depends how short of news they are. I should be grateful. People won't buy books unless they know about them.'

'Did you settle where you're going to stay?'

He nodded, helping himself to the

final slice and breaking off a piece for Banquo, who sat yearningly at his feet, salivating in a disgusting way. 'Brian's an old friend, and he doesn't mind if I take the dog. His yard's fenced.'

She placed her soft hand over his and traced the winding veins. 'I'm going to miss you, David.'

He would have liked her to come, but understood her commitments. He would be away for a week. As well as the business side of the visit, it would be an opportunity to spend time with his father, who would no doubt love to see Banquo again.

His watch said six a.m. David stared at the ceiling, his arm around Cathy as she lay sleeping, her head nestled against his chest. A few months ago he'd been a blocked writer and a bachelor with no intention of settling down. Then along came Cathy. Quiet, unassuming Cathy. He corrected that thought. He'd soon found out she had a mighty temper. He smiled, remembering her stomping along the road in those oversized clothes of his. Yes, a temper, and a generous heart. He'd seen her selfless caring for her grandmother, and her tenderness with small creatures. Here they were, in a funny way an imitation family — he and Cathy, and the two dogs both curled up asleep on the mattress in the corner. He didn't feel restricted or tied down. In fact, he wasn't looking forward to the Sydney trip at all, because Cathy wouldn't be there.

She'd brought something into his life that he hadn't known existed. She wasn't needy, or blaming, or demanding. She was a helpmate, a friend, and a wonderful lover. He'd come alive. And suddenly he was writing again. The words sprang from his refreshed mind, shaping themselves into lines and paragraphs and pages almost by themselves.

Cathy stirred and settled closer. Her cheeks were flushed with warmth, her fair hair in disheveled curls. She looked as defenseless as a child. He could hear birds calling. Flashes of light reflected from the crystal she'd hung to catch the sunlight. He was in a blessed place where there was no need to fret about the future. Whatever problems lay ahead could wait. He should be grateful for happiness. Closing his eyes, he drifted back to sleep.

* * *

The literary luncheon was looming. He'd had no idea it was going to be such a big affair. He'd been staggered to hear the Minister for Arts was attending, probably because there was a push by the government to support culture and heritage — both topics that colored his themes. As his publicity agent had rattled off several other well-known names in literary circles, he felt more and more apprehensive. Where were the pleasant well-heeled ladies who usually attended these functions and carried away their duly autographed book by whoever happened to be speaking on the day?

'What the hell should I wear?'

Cathy smiled as he rummaged through his limited wardrobe. He wasn't a clothes man, but he could hardly turn up in jeans and a T-shirt to address this gathering.

'Don't you have a suit?'

He dragged it out. 'I haven't worn it since the Premier's Awards.'

'I think you'd look lovely in it.' She had a liking for well-groomed, tailored dress.

'I should have had it dry-cleaned.'

'Leave it to me. Have you got an iron?'

'No.'

Cathy laughed at him. 'I think you need a butler.'

'Or a wife?'

'Probably both?' She spoke lightly, ignoring the skip in her heartbeat. 'Let's take a run over to my place. I can sponge and press the suit. What about a shirt?'

'Black?'

'Black tie, white shirt. You're not

225

addressing the Mafia.'

'The way I feel, I won't be addressing anyone.'

'Still nervous?' She hugged him. This was a side of him she'd never seen. How well she understood that shy, insecure feeling, doubting anyone would be interested in your words. In her case, five years with Aaron had well and truly trained her to feel that way. Just recently, she'd realized her own attempt to write had been her way of speaking out. At least on paper, she could express herself.

'Wouldn't you be nervous, Cathy? Politicians, the press, cameras popping . . . It's my idea of hell.'

'I know what. When you start to speak, just put them all out of your mind. Pretend you're talking to me. You know, just the way you've been doing here. Tell me about your books. I'll be there in spirit, anyway.'

David gazed at her silently. 'Mmm. As usual, you're right. I don't have to impress anyone.'

'Can I tell you a tip someone once gave me when I was terrified before an interview?'

'Tell me a tip.' He nuzzled her neck.

'Just imagine the people you're nervous about are all sitting there with nothing on. Starkers. Thin, fat, scrawny, bulging . . . '

He pulled her close and held her. 'You're a wicked wily woman, Cathy Carruthers.'

'I know. Now grab your suit and we'll get you ship-shape for this speech.'

8

Don't think about him bowling down the F3, every minute taking him further away.

Cathy reached for the list of outstanding tasks she'd jotted down. Keep busy. So much of her time had been spent with David that jobs were accumulating.

She'd come to a decision about the nursing course, and had to file her application. A couple of non-urgent computer installations were waiting. Nan's house was due for a thorough spring cleaning, and Pixel needed a bath and flea treatment. Plenty to keep her going.

Her writing was on hold. She no longer felt the need to dream up a fantasy romance. She was smack in the middle of the real thing.

Don't think about him passing that

turnoff where we took a break on Christmas Day.

She prioritized her list, set out the partly filled-in university forms, and ran warm water in the hand basin for Pixel who, knowing her fate, had disappeared. Cathy checked every hiding place she knew of, calling in her most beguiling voice, rattling Pixel's most favored Smacko Strips. Eventually she found the little dog burrowed into the washing in the laundry.

Pixel having been duly washed, dried, brushed and medicated, Cathy checked her list.

Don't imagine him reaching the toll booths, further and further away from me.

She phoned a client and booked in the waiting job. It was at an address near the hospital — an opportunity to fit in Nan's visit.

Her grandmother had reached the restless convalescent stage. Her mind was focused on getting home and planting the late summer annuals, a prospect of such concern to her that Cathy didn't bother arguing. The young social worker, Raeleen, had asked to call a family meeting to discuss Nan's future but Cathy explained there was no family, apart from herself. Nan said she was ready to go home. The hospital said she shouldn't live alone. Cathy was being maneuvered into living with her grandmother, and she wasn't prepared to agree. Surely there must be an alternative?

'What other options does she have?'

'Hostel accommodation, if we can find a place. Services for the aged are so overstretched. Often we have to make do with second best.'

Second best? Not for Nan.

'Assisted living would be ideal. That means someone else in the house with her all the time, and perhaps a weekly home help provided by the department. Could you perhaps . . . '

'I'm starting uni soon.' Cathy spoke up for her point of view. 'I'll be away all day. I'll have shifts at various hospitals, sometimes out of the area.'

Raeleen nodded. And Cathy found as she outlined her hypothetical career change, it took on form and reality. She would become a nurse.

'Your grandmother could sign herself out. But that would remove her from the system, and go against her if she has a further accident.' She stood up. 'Sorry, I have another client waiting now. Old people can be difficult. You have a few weeks to think about it. Meanwhile, I'll start looking into hostel beds and see what's available.'

Cathy returned to the ward to find Nan pacing the corridor, pushing the walker like a recalcitrant child.

'Talking about me?' She nodded to the conference room.

'Raeleen was explaining your options.'

'Very nice of her. Is she planning to inform me? Or do I just get parceled up and posted on?'

'Nan, I know this has been hard.'

'It certainly has been hard!' Her

231

grandmother rarely lost her temper. When it happened, it was a memorable event. Not caring who overheard, Nan thumped the walker along the corridor, Cathy following at a trot.

'Slow down! You're still convalescing.'

'Don't tell me what I am! I don't need young girls running my life. Cathy, you've been wonderful, but I won't be mollycoddled or pushed around. I'm not senile. I can see. I can walk. And I'm going home. I'll get a lawyer if anybody tries to put me away.'

'Nan! Nobody wants to put you away!'

'Huh! What do you call it?' She slammed the walker against the wall, narrowly missing a ward arrangement of gladioli. A large chip of blue paint dropped to the floor and a passing patient skipped out of the way.

'Nan! Calm down, please. You're damaging hospital property.'

'Here's what's going to happen. I'll stay in this wretched place until the doctor says the fracture's fully healed.

Then I'm going home. I want you to open up the place to air, and get me staples. Bread in the freezer. Cartoned milk. Food for Pixel and the animals. Tins of soup. Don't worry, I'll give you the money.'

She was looking flushed. Her lips were set and her eyes were unnaturally bright. Clearly she wasn't to be reasoned with. Cathy could only accept her present attitude and avoid any more confrontation. Raeleen might see Nan as just another difficult old person, but Cathy understood her grandmother's turmoil as she faced the loss of her independence. There must be another alternative to Nan leaving her home and everything that made her life worthwhile. At least Cathy had a few weeks to find it. She hoped.

On the way home, she stopped for a walk along the beach. Usually she shared that time with David and the dogs, chatting with him about their respective days or just enjoying the timeless sensations of sand, sea and the wheeling gulls. Today it was simply lonely. She'd forgotten how to be solitary. He was only in Sydney, but he might as well have been on Mars. He'd promised to phone her as soon as he was settled, but so far her voice mail remained empty. Perhaps there'd be a message on her answering machine at home.

He finally called at nine p.m. when she'd almost given up hope. He said he'd had a hectic day. Brian hadn't mentioned he had a cat, and Banquo had either forgotten his training or had never mastered self-control in regard to hissing felines. He'd had to be tied up in the yard — another obedience lesson he'd decided to forget. To stop his insistent barking, David had walked him all over Darlinghurst and Paddington, until the dog finally conceded defeat and lay scowling at the outraged moggy.

Cathy recounted her unsuccessful visit to Nan, but did not mention her decision about nursing. David wasn't relaxed. It was almost as though his call was just another item on a list. She wanted to tell him she missed him, but sensed he wasn't in the mood for gentle love talk. Perhaps Brian was within earshot. It was always awkward when staying with someone else.

'I'll let you go,' she said, although cutting off contact was the last thing she wanted. 'You sound busy.'

'We're going out for a meal. Brian knows a decent little restaurant, not expensive, he says.'

'You must be starving!' They usually ate by seven.

'I'm in the big city now! Bye, Cathy. Talk tomorrow.' And he was gone. Slowly she put the phone down, hoping the rest of the week would be better than his first day away.

*　*　*

Publicity was part of the job, he knew. His publisher wouldn't appreciate him declaring himself a recluse, unavailable for interviews and book signings. But this week was turning out to be far more stressful than he'd expected. Even as he hit the Sydney traffic, he'd been wishing himself back at home, maybe jogging along the beach or enjoying a casual supper with Cathy. He was discovering she was a woman he could trust. She brought him peace of mind and eased his private fears. The flattery and attention his work sometimes generated was not in her nature. She said what she thought and did not try to manipulate him into making commitments he was not ready for.

Or was he? This relationship was different and he simply couldn't imagine waving a cheery goodbye. A few months ago he'd had his future planned. Travel, usually so exciting a prospect, now felt like an interruption. He was surrounded by unfinished business. His father. The dog. Cathy.

A visit to Gregory only added to his worries. A drizzly rain meant Banquo had to stay in the parking lot, his wet head poking through the back window as he issued forlorn barks. Perhaps he knew his master was near.

Gregory was in his pajamas, lying on top of the quilt, his dim gaze fixed on the window. Today his mood was flat, as though he'd aged ten years.

'What's up, Dad? Why are you still in bed?'

David perched his hip on the edge of the mattress.

'Nothing else to do here.'

'Banquo's in the car. If you get dressed, we could sit out there with him.'

'No thanks, son. All that part of my life has gone. I should get used to it.'

'Tell me what's happened.'

Gregory felt in his bedside drawer and handed David a postcard of a cruise ship.

'Glory's changed her plans. She was offered a special deal by her travel agent. She won't be coming to stay.'

David scanned the perfunctory

words. He felt angry that his thoughtless aunt had caused so much hope and misery, but he wasn't surprised. Glory was one of those people who blundered through life, unaware that her selfish actions had any repercussions. Better his father realized it now, before he upended his life around a forgotten promise.

There was a battering on the door, enough to wake the dead, and a man's impatient voice shouted out: 'This isn't the Hilton, old man. Get your ass down to the dining room if you want any lunch.'

Furious, David wrenched open the door. 'Excuse me? My father's blind, not deaf. I don't like the way you spoke to him.'

The aide was already thumping on a door opposite. 'I'm nobody's slave. We have rules here.'

Intending to say more, David turned at the sound of his father's anxious call. Gregory was beckoning, his gesture almost fearful. 'Don't antagonize him.

It will make things worse.' He lowered his voice. 'Other people have complained. He's under threat of dismissal as it is. And taking it out on all of us. One of those inadequate, power-hungry types.'

'But Dad! It's abuse.'

'A lot of things aren't right. That's life. There's nothing to be done.'

This defeatist attitude was quite unlike his father.

'Are you getting dressed for lunch?' Why did they serve meals at such ungodly hours? It was only eleven fifteen and presumably Gregory had already missed breakfast.

'I can't be bothered,' was all his father said, and would not be cajoled even to come out and pet his beloved dog. David left with a sense of deep unease. Unless something was done, Gregory appeared to be on a downhill slide to death.

The day didn't improve. His publicist had set him up for an interview in *Open Road*, the travel and holiday magazine. The rain had stopped, and a humid fog misted the windscreen. His mind was on his father and he missed the turnoff to North Strathfield. He'd never seen Gregory so low in spirits, not even when he'd been depressed before. The home had deteriorated. Now it was nothing like the facility he'd been led to expect. And that nurse was downright abusive.

Who else could Gregory turn to, if not his only son? But how? David had to work. He couldn't sit at home, his father's carer, and still accept the research grant he'd applied for. Every thought came to a dead end. If only Cathy was here! Her calm voice and lovely face made problems manageable. Surely together they'd find a way to help his father.

A horn blaring in his ear, he switched lanes and managed to get off the motorway. How late was he for the interview? Now it was too hot to leave Banquo in the car. Leashing the restless dog, he saw his trousers were covered in dog hair. He found his way up to the offices, where the receptionist greeted him with surprise.

'Mr. Hillier? We wondered if you were coming. I had no idea you manage all your travel with a guide dog.'

David offered a disarming grin. 'Actually, my vision's A-1. Banquo's my father's dog.' Much petting and admiring ensued before David was shown into a side office where the interview was to be recorded. He sat down, wishing he'd had access to a clothes brush. The interviewer set the recorder going and reeled off a list of personal questions. David's answers were curt, especially when she seemed annoyingly curious about his next project.

'I don't believe in talking about books that haven't happened. It's a good way to kill them.'

He felt thoroughly irritable. The events at the rest home had upset him, he was forced to lug a molting dog all over Sydney in the heat, and the literary luncheon was getting ever closer. What he'd give to be riding the waves on Newcastle Beach . . .

'So what motivates you to write?'

'I've really no idea.'

This wasn't what his publicist had in mind, he knew. Cobbling together some story about the vast outback, man versus nature, the vices and virtues of humanity, he felt guilty as the recorder rolled on. Afterwards he bought a half-cold pie at a local shop and ate it outside, the sun beating on him with Banquo affectionately leaning against him shedding more hair while his saliva dripped onto the pavement.

* * *

The rest of the week brought daily crises. Banquo and the cat escalated their hate relationship. They barked and hissed respectively while Brian, an easygoing sax player, strove to make light of the large dog's apparent desire to swallow his pet whole. Wherever David went he had to take the hot, restless animal, who associated rides in the car with happy walks and games. Banquo seemed to know he was a nuisance, and behaved accordingly. He was no longer a regular working guide dog and his disciplined training was undermined by age and boredom. He whined and itched and scratched, showering the car with a snowstorm of fine hair. David wondered about placing him in a boarding kennel for the next few days but was discouraged by the price, and the fact that most of the places seemed to be so far out of the city. At least Brian, whose gigs were at night, had promised to look after him on the day of the luncheon.

David was marking off his appointments with growing relief. Newcastle and Cathy seemed to be light years away. His phone calls were never timed right. Cathy would be at a client's, or in the bath, or the phone would be in a noisy area and their conversation would resort to 'What did you say?' or 'You're breaking up.' He didn't have the feeling she was missing him, as she rattled off lists of things she had accomplished. She sounded sorrier for Banquo than for him.

'Poor dog! Of course he's unsettled in a strange house, with no games and nothing to do.'

For crying out loud — was she suggesting he tell the press, the MP and the luncheon guests to go hopping while he took Banquo to the beach?

'You sound rather grumpy,' she was adding. 'You've got the lunch thing-o tomorrow. Perhaps you need an early night, instead of carousing around Sydney.'

'Perhaps I do. I'll say goodnight.' How did you slam the phone down on a mobile?

He had a shower, settled the dog on the floor of his bedroom and climbed into the uncomfortable fold-out bunk. Outside, traffic was a steady roar. Through the thin curtain, a streetlight shone straight into his eyes. The ancient rusty fan clattered as it turned. Banquo twitched and snored.

David had decided to go by taxi to the Hyatt. It wasn't far, and if he took his car he'd arrive looking like the abominable snowman. Now the day was here, he felt fatalistic. He'd say his piece, sign the books, smile for the photographers and beat it out of there. All that was left then would be a couple of meetings, one for the TV book program and the other with his publisher. He'd fit in another visit to Gregory, and thankfully head for home.

He dressed, feeling sympathy for city businessmen who had to wear suits in midsummer. He checked his briefcase and tucked in the clothes brush he'd borrowed from Brian. Bribing Banquo with a pig's ear chew, he thanked Brian for dog-sitting and went out to await the taxi. In a few hours this would all be over.

In fact, he felt a stab of excitement as he entered the elegant hotel foyer and was directed to the conference room.

As guest speaker, a fuss was made of him. Smiling strangers offered handshakes, and he was introduced to the main dignitaries in a side room. Delicious aromas wafted in the air. This wasn't going to be hard. He glanced through the wide doors. The beautifully appointed venue, with its rich carpet, floral arrangements, dazzling white napery and glittering cutlery, was already filling with expectant ticketholders. Remembering Cathy's advice, David smiled to himself. Only as a very last resort would he consider visualizing these well-heeled people in their birthday suits.

A hand touched his arm; it was an intimate caress that made him spin around in surprise.

'David! Bet you weren't expecting to see me today?'

Tiffany Murdoch was smiling at him. Of all the people here, she was the only one he was well qualified to imagine in the buff. Their relationship had foundered, like so many others, when the lovely model said she wasn't going mountain-climbing with him in the wilds of the Pilbara. Now she seemed to have recovered from her tears and sulks, not to mention that ghastly scene where she'd threatened to jump off the Harbor Bridge if he wouldn't marry her. She'd been wild and disheveled that night. She certainly made up for it now. Wearing a backless, full-length black gown slit to the thigh, she tipped her lovely face to gaze at him so that he received the full impact of her astonishing green eyes.

'Tiffany, surely your eyes were brown?'

'Intraocular implant, sweetie. People can change, you know!'

He stepped back, wanting to distance himself from the direct fire of her considerable charm.

'Why are you here? I don't remember you as being a great reader.' Fashion magazines and celebrity rags had comprised her intellectual reach, as he recalled.

Picking a thread of Banquo's coat off his lapel, she gave a flirtatious giggle. 'It's an occasion, and I'm one of the beautiful people, in case you've forgotten. I'm here to introduce the speaker. So before I announce you as my ex-lover, I think you'd better bring me up to speed on what I ought to say.'

'Quite so!' said David, alarmed, and he took her by the arm to lead her to a quiet corner. Just as they connected, Tiffany smiling up at him radiantly, the television crew moved in on a close-up of the couple. David, more concerned with briefing his MC, raised his hand in a dismissing gesture and led Tiffany aside, while the cameras continued to flash.

*　*　*

Thank heavens it was over. He'd given his talk. Tiffany had worked the room like a pro, to his relief. Presumably whatever he'd said was appropriate. At least the sea of faces had worn that indulgent, pleased expression accorded a well-liked notable. He'd conversed with the minister, who'd referred to his pending grant application with the kind of nod-and-a-wink tone that implied literary favors could be expected soon. He'd signed dozens of books, nodding and smiling as buyers engaged in hushed confidences about his work, as though he was Solomon dispensing wisdom. How many times had self-doubt made him wonder if people really bothered to read him? A writer worked alone, offering his output to strangers. It would be easy to delude himself, imagining his work was useful. But an occasion like this proved that, out there in the amorphous world, a cross-section of unknown men and women found entertainment and interest in what he had to say. He felt a quiet pride as the last stragglers took their leave.

The reporters and crews had packed up; the minister had excused himself and gone. David and Tiffany were left in the festive room, now being efficiently cleared by hotel staff.

'You didn't eat anything,' Tiffany said.

'I wasn't hungry. A bit nervous, I guess.'

'I didn't eat much either. That dessert looked wonderful, but a girl has to watch her figure.'

'Perhaps there's some place near here where they don't lather cream and chocolate on the food?'

'Why not? Let's catch up. You won't believe this, David. I'm engaged to a hairdresser!' She waved her left hand with its candy-pink nails, and now he saw the solitaire.

'A hairdresser? Well, if it's good enough for the PM, it should be good enough for you.'

They linked arms as they made their way out to the street. They'd always chatted easily, and having lunch with a top model seemed a Sydney sort of thing to do.

Cathy was powering through her list. To placate Nan, she'd evolved the idea of giving the house a spring cleaning. Every day she spent hours wiping down walls, scrubbing out cupboards, washing curtains and vacuuming. She polished the windows till they sparkled and brushed years of dust off the hard-to-reach light shades. Blankets and sheets sagged on the clothesline. Every task seemed to call attention to two more. Nan had once been a meticulous housekeeper, but a major clean-up was beyond her now.

At least if she came home she would find a spotless house waiting for her. And if the worst happened, the place would be ready to be rented or sold.

However, Nan was following this domestic saga as though it was her ticket to freedom. Each time Cathy visited, she found her grandmother waiting expectantly, further lists made out for Cathy to do her bidding.

'Should I have the carpets cleaned, Nan?'

'Why not? There's plenty of money in my pension account. That's the only advantage of being stuck here. It's free.'

'When I soaked the cushion covers they fell to bits. I'll have to buy new ones.'

'I'm glad those drab old things have given up the ghost. Let's have nice new cushions. I don't like those feather pillows either. They were on our bed when Doug was alive. And I've never cared for that dark brown bedspread. We found it in a charity shop, and Doug would have it. That man never could resist a bargain.' She sounded nostalgic.

'Do you still miss him, Nan?' She knew her grandfather had died of a heart attack in his fifties. Nan had been a widow even when Cathy had first come to live with her.

'In a way, dear. Part of your own life dies when you lose the man you love. But time helps. People say that and it's no help at the time. But it's true. The years gallop by and your memories fade.' She turned a sharp glance on Cathy. 'It doesn't pay to dilly-dally, dear. If life happens to offer you a chance, take it!' She did not specify what sort of chance, but it was obvious from her next words that she was talking about David. 'How's that young man of yours?'

'Still in Sydney.'

'I suppose you're missing him.'

'I saw him on TV last night. There was a news item about the lunch.'

'My word! You're moving in fancy circles, going out with a celebrity.'

'He's just an ordinary guy,' Cathy said. She did not add that the footage had shown him with a glamorous girl hanging off his arm. 'Let's finish that list of yours.'

Nan's face lit up. 'It will be so lovely, going home.'

'Has the doctor spoken to you recently?'

'No. That slip of a girl's been back,

going on about me living alone. Cathy . . . ' She gripped her granddaughter's arm. 'You won't let them put me in a rest home, will you?'

Cathy dreaded these conversations. She could see Nan's point. She was alert in mind, and able in body, apart from the accident. All she needed to satisfy the professionals was a companion so that if another incident did occur, she would not be alone and vulnerable.

You'd think there must be thousands of people willing to act in that role. But Cathy's enquiries had led nowhere. It seemed everybody had their private circle of family and friends. The only types who might be available were homeless, or worse — people who might take advantage of Nan in some way. And employing anyone from an agency was out of the question. The rates were far too high.

'Buy me a nice pair of blue towels. The fluffy sort. My old ones are so thin they wouldn't dry a cat. And what about sheets? I put my foot right through one, it's so worn. Find out about thread count. I don't know what it is, exactly, but they go on about it in the home delivery catalogues.'

Cathy stood up. 'I'd better go, Nan. I have to be off to a job early tomorrow. Give me your list and I'll do some shopping afterwards.'

She called into Target on her way home next day and discovered the home decorating section of the store. She'd never spent time like these other customers — intent-looking women who rummaged in sale bins, studying package labels or fingering textures with an experienced touch.

Cathy piled several cushions, a pair of double sheets and the blue towels in her shopping cart, and wandered on through the shop. It must be fun, setting up house with such choice. She'd only brought the bare essentials with her from Melbourne, knowing that wherever she ended up would only be temporary, until she sorted out her life.

What if David ever asked her to move in with him? Would she want to live in his unit? It was nicely situated, but to be honest she'd prefer somewhere with a garden — outdoor furniture, a sun umbrella, a green lawn, maybe flower-beds and a small vegetable plot . . .

Stop nest-building! she told herself. She was dating a celebrity, according to Nan. While she was Cathy Carruthers, computer technician. Nothing more.

* * *

David would head home in the morning. The visit to Sydney had been worthwhile. His publisher was pleased with the publicity and hadn't nagged too hard about the new book. Brian told him there'd been a TV news item about the lunch, which was also mentioned in The Books column of the newspaper. But Gregory was another matter. He was heading back into a bout of depression, and the new staff seemed indifferent. As far as they were concerned, old people did get low-spirited, and no medical intervention was suggested. David was worried. The home had seemed so friendly before it was privatized. He might have to resettle Gregory somewhere else, which would only stir up further stress. Gregory refused to see Banquo, who seemed to know his master was unhappy. The dog paced restlessly whenever he was off his lead, and even turned away from his food.

David decided to take him for a long walk. It was the dinner hour, and dozens of local eateries were doing business with the diverse cross-section of people who patronized these inner city suburbs. Transvestites and flamboyant gays, alcoholics, street kids and homeless tramps mingled with trendy youth and the occasional family group. The city attracted the extremes of human nature. Brian said he loved the action and the variety of Sydney, but David felt the pull of quiet beaches and the rolling surf of home.

Brian was packing his instrument in the car when he got back. 'I'm playing at a footie club, on the way to Blacktown,' he said.

'That's near Dad's rest home.'

'It'll be a late night. Finish around three a.m. I'd guess.'

'I won't wake you in the morning. I plan to get away by six. Brian, thanks for having us. Sorry this fellow's been a pain.'

Brian laughed. 'No worries, mate.'

'Come and stay next time you're up in Newcastle.' The friends shook hands.

Cathy wasn't answering her phone. What a relief it would be to see her in person. Her lovely face and calm manner filled his senses with yearning. He didn't need this flashy life. Cathy understood the simple things in life. She wasn't into the high life or the trappings of success. The week apart had done him good; made him realize he wanted her in his life, permanently. Together they would sort out the problems that faced them both. They would find a way through.

He slept fitfully. Banquo was particularly restless. His whines and pacing woke David several times, until he was tempted to get up and lock the dog in the car for the few remaining hours of the night.

He was just dozing off again when his phone rang. Unable to believe his bad luck, he snatched it up, ready to abuse the prankster or drunk who was dialing him by mistake. Brian's voice came through, concerned.

'Mate? That home your father's in? Listen, I'm driving past, and there's a hell of a commotion going on. Fire engines, ambulances. Looks like a major fire.'

'I'm on it. Thanks.' Leaping out of bed, David dragged on jeans and joggers, grabbed the dog and raced out to the car. His mind filled with flashes of his father, almost blind, stumbling through smoke and flames. He drove wildly through the deserted suburbs, seeing a sinister red-orange glow in the sky as he approached the home. How incredibly lucky Brian had been in the area.

It was impossible to get any parking on the grounds. Several fire trucks were already hosing water jets towards the blaze, while ambulances received smoke-blackened patients being carried on stretchers from the building. Somehow the news had reached other families who were milling around in frantic groups, trying to intercept anyone with news about their relatives. Firemen were holding guard at the doors, refusing entry, while their colleagues inside crawled or stumbled through the dense smoke, trying to rescue those still trapped inside. Those who could walk were helped out into the grounds, and others were carried one way or another, while rumors spread that many had not escaped.

Banquo was frantic. As David opened the boot to leash him, he took a flying leap to freedom and raced straight past the guards, disappearing inside the building. David tried to chase him but was pulled up by an adamant fireman.

'You can't go in. Sorry, mate. Stand out of the way please.'

David began to search the car park, hoping to see Gregory somewhere. Small groups of miserable, shocked patients were gathered at checkpoints, awaiting transport to other facilities. A few were bed-ridden, still with IV drips and disconnected oxygen masks dangling around their smutty forms. Those who had suffered burns were in the worst pain, crying helplessly in confusion. David remembered the talk that others were still inside. He felt sick. What a terrible way to die. Was his father one of those? He would never forgive himself, if so. He had chosen this place, and look at the outcome. He was bereft.

Perhaps there was another entrance? Pushing through the preoccupied crowd, he ran down a narrow side path to an asphalt yard that served the commercial waste collection bins, laundry and delivery supplies. So far the fire hadn't taken hold of this area. Infiltrating smoke poured from open doors, but the sheds and outhouses were relatively secure. Desperately he began to search, calling his father's name.

9

Flames spurted from the main building, punctuated by intermittent crashes as beams and roof tiles collapsed. A hideous glow illuminated the night sky, and the pungent smell of burning filled David's nostrils. His eyes watered as he breathed in the soupy, smoke-polluted air. If he was choking, how must it be for the weak residents still caught in that inferno? The firemen were working to capacity, their team spirit evident as they broke in through accessible doors and windows not yet consumed by the blaze. Again and again a rescue was attempted, at what risk to themselves nobody knew. At any moment the entire roof might cave in. The cost in lives had yet to be known. Already a few shrouded forms lay on gurneys in the waiting ambulances, and more were likely to follow as weak lungs and hearts succumbed to the stress of the event.

David had searched the back yard without result. He ran on, following the path, hoping against hope there might still be another open door. By the time he had rounded the building his hopes were sinking fast. Surely nobody inside that inferno could possibly be alive? His good intentions in placing Gregory here must have resulted in his dad's premature, terrible end. How would he ever be able to forgive himself?

He came to the detached courtyard where dementia sufferers liked to sit and enjoy the garden views. Its wide glassed windows overlooked lawns and trees. Peering in, David thought he saw movement. Yes, somebody was inside! He thought he heard a feeble cry for help. The only door was padlocked. He had no hope of breaking the lock. The windows were the only other option. He had nothing strong enough to smash through that tough glass. Frantic, he looked around. All he could see was a wrought-iron garden seat. He dragged it over and, with the strength of desperation, hurled it at the window. The toughened surface shattered but did not break. He tried again and again, discovering he could draw on a power he did not know he possessed. With a final blow, he broke the glass wide open and clambered through the opening.

'Thank God!' he heard Gregory say, as Banquo guided him to the escape hole and David pushed man and dog to safety. So far, the area had been insulated from the worst of the smoke. The three figures, smutty and soot-blackened but unharmed, took shelter at a distance, while the hungry flames continued to devour the home.

David looked closely at his father. He seemed to be in good shape, consider-ing his ordeal. He said he'd been trying to find an alternative escape route after realizing the front entrance was impass-able. He'd wandered about, confused, and had almost given up when Banquo appeared out of nowhere and led him to the courtyard.

'I thought it was a miracle,' said Gregory, his arm around the panting dog.

The night was rent with men's shouts, the cries of frightened patients and the shrill sirens of the backup fire brigade and departing ambulances. The home had catered to over eighty patients, who now had no place to go. Hospitals were on alert, dividing up the casualties, but the system had no way of accommodating such an influx. A few families had relatives who had escaped first and were unharmed. A staff member was arguing with a determined man who said he was taking his mother home with him at once.

'Everyone must be accounted for and given a medical check,' said the harried nurse. Ignoring her, the man swept his mother up in his arms and put her in his car.

David regarded his father.

'Dad. I need you to be honest with me. Do you need to see a doctor right away?'

'I'm one of the lucky ones. No burns. That courtyard saved me from the smoke. I reckon I'm fine.'

'We have two choices. You can be taken to hospital from here, or you can come back to Newcastle and see a doctor in the morning.'

Gregory managed a laugh. 'Would I rather sit in some overworked emergency department for the rest of the night, or go home? What do you reckon, son?'

'I'll go and let the staff know you're safe.' David stood up, finding he was weak in the legs.

'Keep clear of that male aide if he's hanging about,' Gregory advised. 'He's probably here, enjoying the scenery.'

'What do you mean?'

'He got the sack. Went round telling everyone he was going to burn the place to the ground.'

'What?'

'We all thought it was a bluff. Now, I wonder . . . '

'There'll be an investigation. If it was

arson, and he was responsible, he'll serve a good prison sentence for manslaughter.'

'Let's get out of here. Give me an arm up.' Gregory hauled himself upright with David's help. 'At least one good thing's come out of this. I'm going home.'

Without bothering to pick up his gear from Brian's, David drove straight to the freeway. His suit and other goods could wait. He would obviously have to make a return trip to Sydney to arrange transfer papers and anything else that aged care services would need to resettle Gregory. Meanwhile, the family house remained empty. David would simply move in with his father until proper accommodations could be arranged.

He felt a huge sense of reprieve. Refugees must feel like this, escaping the dread of imprisonment and torture for some unspecified crime. It didn't matter if you walked away with nothing; at least you were free. In David's case, free of the guilt he would have carried if Gregory had died.

Considering the ordeal he'd been through, his father was remarkably chipper. Like Banquo, he was filthy; cinders and smuts marked his pajamas and the pungent stench of smoke pervaded the car. In the back of the car, the Labrador lay in a state of exhausted peace, reacting to the stress his aging body had endured as he must have searched the burning building for his master. He would need a check-up, but David did not think he was at any serious risk. The rest of the day would be busy. He'd have to move some of his belongings into the old house and shop for supplies. Gregory had to see a doctor and Banquo needed a trip to the vet.

And Cathy. They'd spoken last night but that phone call seemed to be in another lifetime. She was expecting him home this morning, but hardly under these circumstances. Home? Since when had he felt such attraction in that word? He was a rolling stone. Or had that stone finally come to a halt, its restless journey ended?

They'd planned to meet for a welcome lunch at her place, but he knew in her calm, understanding way, she would set aside her plans and step in to help with his immediate needs. There would be no cross-examinations, no demands. Imagining her warm, open smile and comforting hug, he unconsciously accelerated, needing to close the distance between them.

★   ★   ★

Cathy was planning a simple yet special meal for lunch: quiche, a tossed salad, fresh rolls and a crisp white wine, followed, she guessed, by a reunion in the bedroom. She'd changed the sheets, spraying them with touches of perfume. Showered, her hair washed and blow-dried, and wearing her new set of lacy red underwear, she pulled on casual wear and applied a touch of lip gloss.

She didn't need blusher — her thoughts had brought a pink glow to her cheeks — and she knew whatever she put on her face would end up smeared all over the pillows if her fantasies were accurate. She imagined him striding in, dark hair a little awry, with that confident walk that seemed to say *Here I am!*, sweeping her into his arms, pulling her close. His want for her would be immediate, hard and urgent; delighting in her feminine power, she would press against him, teasing. The contours of their bodies would interlock like jigsaw pieces, made to fit.

How would their union be? Tender or rough? Sexy or playful? She loved the way he led her out of her natural reserve, inviting her to forget all inhibition and share his desire as natural and right.

Later they would talk. He would tell her about his week away. She had her own news for him. But that could wait till they were lying drowsily in each other's arms, drained, all passion spent. She would go to the bathroom and freshen up, then make coffee the way he liked it, and carry the mugs back to bed. What if it would only be mid-afternoon of a working week where most people were out in the world, earning their wage? Cathy and David would make their own world, away from practical concerns.

And when they did get up to face reality, they would do whatever had to be done together, hands clasped, bodies and souls united.

There was an hour or so to fill in before David was likely to be in Newcastle. Settling on the couch with Pixel on her lap, she flipped channels to the twenty-four-hour news and sat startled as a 'Breaking News' headline ran across the bottom of the TV. Nursing home fire. Multiple deaths confirmed.

Magnolia Gardens? Wasn't that David's father's rest home?

She leaned closer. The footage

showed a chaotic scene of leaping flames, milling watchers and evacuees being loaded into ambulances. Just for a moment she thought she saw a man very like David in the throng, but the image was gone before she could be sure.

Grabbing her phone, she dialed his number, but the call rang unanswered.

With a sense of deep unease, she prepared to wait. Whatever was going on, she would find out soon enough, but something told her that her plans for a romantic day were not to be.

When his knock sounded, she literally ran along the hall, Pixel barking at her heels, to welcome him. She only needed one glance at the sorry trio of dirty, disheveled visitors to confirm the worst. All she could do was welcome them inside. David's father was in filthy pajamas; Banquo's sooty coat told her he'd played a major role in the rescue, while David looked exhausted.

Her nature resorted to calm in the face of an emergency. Running in top gear, her mind swiftly prioritized needs. Of the three, Banquo looked to be in the worst state, panting and moving wearily, though the sight of Pixel seemed to lift his spirits. The dog required immediate veterinary care. The aged man appeared quite sprightly. A shower and change of clothes seemed to be his pressing need.

Her gaze met David's, trying to convey such unspoken concern that he returned a grateful smile.

'I couldn't phone you,' he said. 'I left my mobile at Brian's. It was such a rush.'

'Of course. I saw the news. Tell me later. I'm making tea now, while you just ring around and get an appointment for him.' She nodded to the dog, at present lapping like a parched desert traveler at Pixel's water bowl. He drank the refill she offered, and sagged down on the floor near Gregory as though his body felt too heavy to hold up.

Refreshed by tea and warm bread rolls, David departed with Banquo.

Gregory accepted a refill of his cup, and a second round of eats. He almost seemed to be enjoying the drama of his rescue, though he had yet to learn that several of his fellow inmates had not escaped the blaze.

'How could it have happened?' Cathy was bewildered. One could imagine derelict buildings catching fire, but surely fire doors and sprinklers would have been installed in a public building?

'My bet is arson. One of the staff, an unpleasant fellow, got the sack. Several of us heard him ranting, saying he'd burn the place to the ground. Of course we took it as an idle threat.'

Cathy realized there would be an investigation. Gregory's evidence sounded vital. But for now, his need appeared to be a shower and change of clothing. As far as she could judge, he had enough vision to move about. His misty eyes had already examined her and, in a gallant manner, he'd said he remembered her.

'Can you manage by yourself?' She

showed him to the bathroom. Not wanting to offend his dignity, she added, 'I'm going to be a nurse, you know.'

'And a thoroughly kind one, I can tell. Just give me the soap and shampoo and lay out the towels. I'll be fine.'

She made sure the water temperature was adjusted and left him to it while she sorted out something he could wear. When David returned an hour later, he was faced with the unusual sight of his father in a pair of pink pajamas adorned with teddy bears.

'Where's Banquo?' Gregory sounded alarmed.

'The vet decided to keep him in for observation overnight. Don't worry, Dad. He's fine. It's just a precaution because of his age. He inhaled a bit of smoke; nothing serious, but he's an old dog. We'll get settled into the family house and collect him tomorrow.'

'That'll do nicely. Sit down, son. You sound beat.'

'You do.' Cathy's heart went out to

David. He'd been running on high alert for many hours. Now the emergency had passed, his body was tired. She guessed he wanted nothing more than to lie down on a soft bed and sleep. But there was so much still to see to.

Cathy's firm hand was insisting he sit back on the sofa. Quietly she handed him a plate of quiche and salad so appetizing that, automatically, he began to eat. When he'd finished she removed the plate and handed him a glass of fruit juice.

Making a huge effort, he scrambled to his feet. 'I should get moving.' His speech sounded slowed down, as though his brain refused to cooperate with his limbs.

'You are going to bed!' Ignoring his argument, she tugged his arm.

'I have to . . .'

'Sleep,' she finished for him. 'Your father and I are going to have a nice quiet lunch together. I've already arranged a doctor's appointment for him late this afternoon.'

'I might just grab a ten-minute nap,' he mumbled as he collapsed onto the scented sheets and sank into a two-hour slumber.

* * *

Gregory and Cathy struck up an easy friendship. Pixel had taken a liking to the visitor, pawing at his leg to be picked up and cuddled. He was a natural dog lover, earning instant brownie points with Cathy. Naturally the fire was foremost in their minds, but the talk gradually turned to other issues. Cathy enjoyed his sharp insights and occasional wit.

'You remind me of my grandmother.' She was paying him a compliment.

'Yes, you mentioned her when you visited at Christmas. Is she out of the hospital?'

'Not yet. They don't think she should live alone.'

'And what does she have to say about that?' A dry smile lifted his mouth.

'I won't repeat it! You see, she was in the house alone when she fell. If I hadn't gone there . . . ' Her lip quivered at the memory of Nan, unable to summon help.

Gregory gave a sympathetic sigh. 'Who was it who said, 'Old age is not for sissies'? We get moved around and put here and there, and there's nothing we can do about it.'

'My grandmother's certainly putting up a fight.'

'Good for her! I hope she finds a solution.'

'She's mobile again. The rehab hospital told me I could take her out for a drive now. You'll probably meet her.'

'I'd like that.'

Cathy filed that away. A visit to Gregory and David would be ideal. She'd been dreading the moment when Nan demanded to be driven to her own home. Cathy was sure that once inside, her grandmother would barricade the door and refuse all future help, which would harm her full recovery and set up further problems for the future.

Cathy saw very little of David for the next week. Services to the family home had to be reconnected, provisions bought, and David's essentials shifted from his apartment. Gregory had been given the all-clear. The doctor had written him new prescriptions for his diabetes and given his lungs and breathing capacity a careful assessment. He said the diabetic retinopathy, the cause of his legal blindness status, was stable. Gregory's central vision was blurry, but he compensated by using peripheral sight, and for everyday activities was still managing well. Of course the elderly man had not escaped a reaction to the traumatic fire. The news reports confirmed loss of life and suspicion of arson, and Gregory was one of those who'd heard the verbal threats and would be interviewed by the police. He was concerned about Banquo, who hadn't been released from veterinary care as quickly as expected. When David was summoned to Sydney to report on his father's whereabouts and discuss his options, he asked Cathy if she'd mind calling in at the old home.

'Dad's wandering about, at a bit of a loss. Some dream he's been hanging on to has gone. Things aren't the same without Mum. I think he'd forgotten how lonely he became, last time he tried living by himself.'

'Of course I'll visit. I can help him with his meds, maybe cook a meal.'

'I'll be back tomorrow. Banquo will be ready for discharge. Cathy, thanks for being there. You've been a huge support.'

'It's nothing. I'm happy to help out.'

But she was starting to feel over-loaded. Added to Nan's menagerie and the daily visits to the rehab center, she still had to pay the rent. Her backlog of repair work was building up and she'd been called in for an interview after filing her application for the nursing course. She was happy to visit Gregory, but if only there were more hours in the day. Her intimacy with David had been replaced with quick phone calls and worrying news. Of course nobody lived in a fool's paradise of romance forever. But those moonlit beach walks, special dinners and breathtaking lovemaking were just a memory.

This was life with David. He led the way, called the shots, and she followed. A hint of her past with Aaron? Was she fatally drawn to men whose issues were too pressing to ever consider her own direction? There was a reason why David was still a bachelor at thirty-five. He'd hinted at many past entanglements which had ended.

She sat stroking Pixel. What would she say if David asked her to forget her business and her dream of nursing and join him on his research trip? The idea of travel was exciting. She would have a difficult choice to make. Meanwhile there were so many unresolved matters — Nan, Gregory, Banquo. This must be maturity. Her carefree youth had somehow never happened. Already she was supposed to make difficult decisions on behalf of others who depended on her.

Loading Pixel and a simple macaroni and cheese she had prepared for supper, she drove to Gregory's house. It was an old weatherboard home, 1930s style, probably charming when its gardens were in order and its paintwork maintained. At present it looked unkempt. The lawn was a foot high, the flowerbeds were a choked mess of weeds, and the fountain was full of rotting leaves. As she made her way past the tendrils of wisteria on the porch, they clutched and clung as though warning her she'd never get away.

Gregory welcomed her, his expression lightening as he noticed Pixel. 'Ah, the little one! You follow me. I've got a treat for you.'

'I hear Banquo's coming home tomorrow.' Cathy followed him to a kitchen so dim she could barely see. 'May I turn on the light, Gregory?'

'Is it off?' He found a dog treat which Pixel found acceptable after cautious inspection. 'I'm sorry. I live in a twilight world. What have you brought in that dish you're carrying? It smells delicious.'

'Just macaroni and cheese.'

'Ah! One of my favorites. Molly was a great cook, you know. Always on the go. Garden used to be best on the street. I suppose it's overgrown now?'

'A bit.' Poor old man, she thought. One never did expect good things to change.

'We'll eat in the conservatory. Molly and I liked to sit there, among her ferns and houseplants. She had a magnificent variety. You'll see.' He produced plates and cutlery, peering into cupboards and drawers while she waited.

'I'll carry them out,' she offered, unobtrusively wiping away a few marks with the tea towel. The conservatory turned out to be a dingy room, its glass windows so dirty that the light struggled through. Potted plants of dead stalks formed a sad parade.

'There's Molly's orchids. What do

you think of them?'

'They're not in flower,' was all she could tactfully tell him.

'Probably not the season. Well, sit down, young lady. Make yourself at home.'

Cathy perched on a dusty cane chair whose cushions wore old stains that suggested a bird must have been trapped in the conservatory at some time.

'David doesn't know what he's missing.' His filmy gaze held hers as he chuckled.

'He had to tidy up affairs in Sydney.'

'Always on the move, that boy.'

'You don't think he'll ever settle down?' She didn't want to hear his answer.

Gregory surprised her with his regretful words. 'It's probably my fault, Cathy. I was one of those men — a scientist — always seeking and pushing boundaries. I encouraged David to be like me. Do better. Go higher. Aim to be the best. Molly used to say to me,

'Leave the boy alone! Let him find his own way.' I didn't listen. Men didn't, back then. Yes, I know, it's surprising to a young slip like you. Men expected women to mind their place and be homebodies, waiting for when their man came home.'

'I don't think all marriages were like that,' said Cathy, smiling as she thought of Nan. 'Perhaps you should have a debate with my grandmother!'

'I'd like that! Bring her to lunch, my dear. We'll have a ding-dong go together.'

'She'd enjoy that. She's itching to go home.'

'Of course. They send us off to rest homes. But we don't want rest! We need challenge and occupation just like you, my dear.'

'I can understand.' She glanced at her watch. 'Shouldn't you have your insulin before we eat?'

'Ah, David primed you! Yes. Mustn't forget. Don't want any drama, do we? You have a look at those photos while I get the gear.'

He left Cathy behind to take in the depressing environment, where neglect had erased all traces of home. Poor David! He must hate living here. She hoped he'd find a solution to suit everyone. Now Gregory was home, he would resist institutional care. It was David's problem. She had to sort out Nan's future. Setting it all in the *too hard to deal with* basket, she leafed through the photo album on the table. Many of the pictures showed David at various stages of growth, displaying sports banners and awards while his proud parents applauded. Cathy had never known doting love. Now, turning the pages, she realized there was a price to everything. Deep within the handsome man she cared for resided this small boy, always taking risks and pushing himself to greater achievement. Against such a drive, she felt powerless. She couldn't hold him back.

★ ★ ★

Nan was surprisingly vain. When Cathy passed on the invitation to lunch, her grandmother looked aghast.

'You'll have to get my hair dye and help me do my roots. I can't possibly meet Mr. Hillier looking like this.'

'He's half blind! He won't see what color your hair is.'

'Doesn't matter. I'll see. I want you to bring in that blue dress I bought on sale. And my white earrings. And shoes. I'm not going out to lunch in slippers.' She stared in disgust at the hated walking stick. 'I'll have to take that wretched thing. I'll look like some old woman falling in the grave.'

'Nan! You're not going on a date.'

'You laugh all you like. You just never know what's around the corner. You've told me quite a bit about your young man's father. I like the sound of him.'

'He's very nice. Well-educated. Polite. A thorough gentleman.'

'And a widower, you say.'

'Nan!'

'Don't worry. I don't want another

husband. Just bring in my things. And don't forget the dye. Just a light brown, to freshen up. I don't want to look like Jezebel.'

★ ★ ★

The lunch was arranged for the following weekend. Cathy used her spare time reducing her list of outstanding jobs. Her nursing interview went well, and she felt even more certain this was the right path for her. There might be a vacancy in the next entering class, and she walked back to her car through the university grounds, feeling confident her name would be among those accepted for the course.

She'd finished her spring clean of Nan's home. The simple house was transformed. Light flowed through the polished windows, the carpets released a pleasant scent, and clean and modern fabric replaced the shabby curtains and cushion covers. Cathy had scrubbed out and re-lined the kitchen cupboards and defrosted the fridge. The gardener she'd paid for a day's work had transformed the exterior. The lawns were trimmed, the garden beds dug over.

She could clean and tidy all she liked, but the outstanding problem was unresolved. Her talk with Gregory only reinforced Nan's point of view. She simply wasn't ready to sell her home and turn her back on life, accepting dependent living. At Cathy's time of need, Nan had opened her heart and her home to a difficult teenager. It might be time to return that favor, even if Cathy's dream of nursing had to be put on hold. She longed to talk over her dilemma with David, but every day brought some new problem he was dealing with.

'When can we get together privately?' she asked when he phoned her.

'I know. It's been so difficult. But Banquo's home, and Dad's fairly settled. A detective came and spoke with him today. I want to see you,

Cathy. Can I come this evening? Unless you're busy?'

Busy! Already her mind was racing into overdrive. Surely an evening in his arms would lay to rest her fear that, like a wild horse, he would not be confined.

★   ★   ★

Pixel heard the car pull up and raced to the front door. Following her, Cathy felt wired. There were rare moments in life when everything changed. Somehow she knew tonight would be one of those times. The pressure of recent weeks had tried to divide them. David was pulled one way by his father, his work, the research grant. And equally strong claims — her grandmother, her own career change — tugged Cathy in an opposite direction. Life was conspiring to keep them apart, his restless nature tearing him away from her.

David was at the door, wearing the same cream chinos and black T-shirt he'd had on the first time they'd met.

Tall, somehow imposing, his wavy black hair in disarray, he seemed to take over her space. She almost took a step back. He was smiling, impatient to show her the envelope in his hand.

'I stopped to pick up my mail. I've got the grant!'

Her heartbeat faltered. However happy he might be, her body said this was bad news for her. She continued to hold the door open while he stepped inside on a waft of aftershave. Even as she felt drawn by the attractive spicy scent, she sensed his mind was elsewhere and pulled away, not wanting a distracted embrace.

'That's great news.' She tried to cover her flat response.

'I can finally sort out my plans. I've got a lot to tell you.'

Cathy led the way to the sitting room. This was nothing like the private reunion she'd imagined. A month ago, the simple things had felt so special. Walks along the beach. A quiet meal together. Lovemaking in his bed, or hers, where he teased her nipples erect or buried his face between her breasts. She wished they didn't have to discuss important plans. She'd much rather simply sit and talk.

'Do you want a glass of wine?'

'I see you started without me.' He smiled, indicating the half-empty glass.

'Yes or no?'

He picked up on her sharp tone.

'Anything wrong?'

'Of course not.'

He reached for the wine bottle, filled a glass and tossed back a gulp. Handing her the letter from the Literature Board, he drained the rest of the drink.

'Read it! They've given me more than I expected. I'll have time to do a thorough job and dig back further into history than I was planning. That way, the book will have more depth. I'm hoping it will be my best ever.'

She felt deflated. Remembering this was what David wanted, she just felt empty. And puzzled. Surely he didn't plan to simply take off, leaving his

father and Banquo to fend for themselves?

'What about Gregory?'

'Oh. That's all worked out well. I had
a meeting with the liaison people in
Sydney. A new home in Canberra will
take able-bodied residents.'

'Canberra? Does your father know
anybody there?'

'Not as such. He'll make friends, in
time.'

'Really? What about Banquo?'

'I've been making preliminary enquiries through the guide dog people. They
say they can place him as a companion
animal.'

'Where?'

'Wherever there's a place for him, I
suppose.'

'I suppose you mean Brisbane? Or
maybe Adelaide?'

'Wherever. Is this a cross-
examination?' David reached for the
bottle to top up his wine glass. 'I don't
suppose you've got any nibbles? Now,
here's the very best part. Will you come

with me?' He reached over and seized her hand. 'Cathy, I'm asking you to be part of my life.'

'Part of your life?' Carefully she detached her hand from his grip. 'In West Australia?' Coldly she stood up, looking down on him as though he was a particularly nasty dropping Pixel had deposited on her quilt.

Her remote expression startled him. 'Why are you looking at me like that?'

'This is where you and I part company, David. I'm sorry, but I think you're the most selfish man I've ever met.'

10

Cathy in a rage was quite a sight. Now her sensitive mouth quivered, her cheeks were flushed, and her eyes were the color of an angry sea.

'So let me just recap. Your plan is to dump your father back in a nursing home and send Banquo interstate to some new owner you haven't even met. If you can live with that, good luck! Oh yes, I drop my plans to become a nurse and follow you wherever you happen to go. Of course there's no room in all this for a home, or children. But then we wouldn't be married, would we? Well, I'm sorry. Your plans don't happen to coincide with mine.'

Plenty of women had thrown a scene when it came to the point of his leaving. He was almost used to the histrionics. Except that every word Cathy said was stinging with the bitter lash of truth.

She wasn't just making claims for herself. She was defending the vulnerable, an old man and a faithful dog who deserved better than he was proposing.

Still she scowled at him, her lips set, her eyes red and glistening with unexpressed tears. She was about to say goodbye. He knew it; he could feel the words forming in her mind.

'Cathy!'

She paused, hands on her hips as though impatient for him to go.

'I'm sorry. You're right. We need to talk.'

'You might need to talk. I have nothing to say to you. You should go.'

He stood up, intending to embrace her, but she flung off his touch. 'Leave me alone! I should be grateful you've shown me the kind of man you really are. Please go.'

Nothing he could say was going to reach her in this mood. Without another word, he walked away; Pixel followed him along the hall and, with a puzzled expression, watched as he went out and closed the door.

He missed his footing on the step and almost fell. He grabbed the rail, sucking in a few deep breaths to try and clear the dizzy feeling. His body felt as if it was coming apart.

He made it to the car and fumbled the key in the ignition, but did not drive away yet. The lights of Cathy's window glowed invitingly, but he was no longer welcome in her home. He'd lost the woman he loved. There, he'd admitted it, and now he'd never get a chance to tell her.

Sadness overwhelmed him. His head felt too heavy to hold up. Clasping his hands like a pillow on the steering wheel, he slumped forward, resting his forehead there.

★   ★   ★

So that was that. A chapter ended. Whatever David did was no longer her concern. Anger held back the tide of sorrow that was rising like a tsunami far out to sea. She would not be swamped by sadness and self-pity. Forget love. The price David had outlined was too high to consider. She needed to believe she was living a good life, doing her bit for others. Happiness would never come at the price he had so casually named.

She would see out the last few duties, get through the lunch with Gregory, be honest with the nursing board about her commitments, and move in with Nan. No, it wasn't what she wanted. But she realized she could not place her lively, active grandmother in care. It was far too soon. One day, yes, that decision would have to be made. Then she would follow her dream and work full-time as a nurse. Why, if she wasn't too old by then, she might find work in some of those same remote regions David's books described. How ironic that would be.

Pixel was standing at her feet, looking up at her. It seemed the one friend she could rely on tonight was this tiny creature whose only ambition was to offer love. Cathy scooped her up and hugged her close, as a damp pink tongue licked concernedly at the salt of her falling tears.

★ ★ ★

'You look lovely, Nan!' Cathy did a double-take at the sight of the attractive woman waiting to be taken out to lunch. Smartly dressed in a fitted blue dress, her hair subtly colored and waved, and with tasteful makeup enhancing her fine skin and alert eyes, Nan sprayed on a light perfume reminiscent of sweet peas, and smiled.

'Don't write me off as an old fogey yet, Cathy. I wonder what we're having for lunch? I'm so tired of hospital food.'

'Something special.' So David had promised. He'd phoned her several times, ostensibly about the catering, but she'd replied in monosyllables and kept the calls as short as possible. So far, she'd said nothing to Nan about her break-up with him. Why spoil this day out?

After today, she would probably not see David again. She accepted their romance was over. Why prolong the pain? Let him get on with his arrangements by himself. She felt so sad for Gregory and Banquo, but it wasn't in her power to intervene. Perhaps one day she would see David's name on a new dust jacket, and think back to the brief, passionate affair they'd shared. After all, she'd been miserable over Aaron a few short months ago. Now he was simply a figure in her past. Somehow it was hard to imagine the memory of David would ever fade like that.

He'd reached her, explored her needs, crashed through her self-imposed barriers and lifted her to ecstatic heights of union. It was so hard to believe they would never wander a quiet beach hand-in-hand again. Never share those walks on the sand, Pixel scampering like a tiny rocking horse,

Banquo plowing through the shallows, sniffing seaweed and investigating smelly detritus washed up by the tide.

Never laugh together at some ironic joke.

Never make love again.

'Come on, let's go.' She couldn't bear these flashes of regret continually swamping her at the most unlikely moments. 'And bring your stick.'

Nan grumbled, but accepted that a walking stick was the price of independence. 'Let's stop at the bottle shop and get a nice port.'

'But you don't drink.'

'Not often. But gentlemen enjoy a port, dear.' Nan shook her head. 'Really, Cathy, you have a lot to learn.'

* * *

Gregory was also done up to the nines in a dress suit and polished shoes, and liberally daubed with David's aftershave. He greeted Nan graciously, obviously taken by her presentation and dress.

'Blue, I think? My favorite color. Do come in. The young ones have told me so much about you.'

'I've been incarcerated for months, Mr. Hillier. So thank you for the invitation.'

'You must call me Gregory.'

They were away, chatting like old acquaintances, while David hovered in the kitchen and Cathy stood apart, glancing at titles in the well-stacked bookshelves. Gregory might not be able to read these days but he was obviously an erudite man with wide-ranging interests. She turned away, resisting the image of a little boy gazing up at all those tomes, perhaps wondering if he too might one day earn a place there.

She could hear Nan and Gregory breaking the ice with introductions.

'Joy? Well, fancy that. My mother's name was Joy.'

Cathy walked out to the conservatory. The photograph album Gregory had shown her still lay on the table there. She turned the mounted pages and again the small boy gazed out at her, holding his trophies. He did not look particularly proud or happy; rather, he seemed to be offering his prizes to someone out of the picture. His father?

How ironic! This ingrained need to achieve was the very thing driving him to the far extremes of Australia, and Gregory back into a rest home.

Still, she had made a rational decision to avoid a disastrous mistake. She and David just weren't compatible. On the surface, sure, they had so much in common; but when it came to values, they were streets apart. She accepted that. Then why did she feel so fluttery, just knowing he was near? She must be imagining the magnetic pull that tugged at her heart, wanting to go and speak to him and find some miracle had changed him. Not likely — setting out to change someone was Mission Impossible.

David was a strong man. He believed in his work. He was in no doubt that his father needed rest home care. As far as he was concerned, Banquo was just an animal and needed nothing more than kind care. He simply wasn't the nurturing kind.

Whereas she was. There was nothing more to say.

Good aromas drifted from the kitchen when she walked inside. Gregory and Nan sat in opposite chairs, inclined towards each other, two port glasses and the bottle between them on the low table. They were comparing musical tastes, Gregory vigorously defending Bach and Nan saying she was an Abba fan. They barely noticed Cathy as she found herself drawn irresistibly towards David. He was tossing a green salad at the bench.

'Can I help?' It felt impossible to refer to their last meeting.

'Thanks. I think it's under control. It's a pre-cooked lasagna and something called apple danish. Dad likes it.'

'I could whip the cream.'

'Good. I'm almost ready to serve.'

This was possibly the last time she would ever spend with him. A polite exchange as though they were fellow chefs was ludicrous.

'Nan's getting on very well with Gregory.'

His firm mouth relaxed into a smile. 'So I hear. Just like a courting couple! It wouldn't surprise me to see them go walking out arm in arm.'

'David? Perhaps you and I should go for a walk after lunch?'

She was expecting a chilly rebuff. All he said was, 'Okay. Can you carry in those plates?'

She was oblivious to the meal, eating mechanically while she anticipated the last words they would ever say to each other. Her mind raced over variations of sadness, love, loss, hurt, confusion and final parting. Fortunately Nan and Gregory carried the conversation, sharing a note of black comedy in their stories of recent confinement. Their talk moved on to love of dogs, opinions of certain movie actors Cathy had never heard of, and a code of repartee that made Cathy suspect this was how old-fashioned flirtation got underway.

'Are you taking Banquo for a walk?' asked Gregory after lunch, but Cathy shook her head. Already tears pricked her eyes and she knew she would need all her self control to remain calm and sensible. She did not want to share David on this last outing. Not even with a dog.

*   *   *

David knew this suburb well. It was an orderly crisscross of streets occupied by older homes and gardens. Why had Cathy suggested this walk? She seemed to have nothing to say, just put one foot in front of the other as though on a forced exodus. Her face looked closed; her mouth was down-turned, her gaze set on the pavement ahead. He'd better get on and say what he wanted her to hear, now. If she shut down again, he might never have a chance to reach her.

He'd changed during those long, sleepless nights when he'd replayed their angry scene. Her scathing words had been too close for comfort, at first. But gradually he'd taken them on board. She was too honest to be manipulating him. She told it like it was. And he'd heard her.

He'd made wrong assumptions about his father. Living together, he'd seen Gregory was still active and capable. Sure, he needed help with the fine print; things like remembering his medication. Mentally, Gregory was just as alert as his son. They'd chatted just last evening. That potted history he'd delivered on the pearling industry was detailed and accurate — hardly the words of a dementia sufferer.

'White pearling masters arrived in the 1860s, using Aboriginals as slaves. Once helmets and suits were standard equipment, the Chinese and Japanese joined the lugger fleets. Then Malays, and men from Timor and the Philippines. It was a hazardous life.'

He'd moved on to outline the health risks, from the bends to encounters with manta rays and box jellyfish. David listened, realizing that vegetating with Alzheimer's sufferers and the dying would depress any normal man. As for Banquo, he'd given his whole existence to serve Gregory and risked his life to bring him from the fire. Cathy was right. The old dog deserved to live out his remaining years contentedly.

What had Cathy meant about children, marriage, a home? She'd never hinted, like other women, that she expected a big diamond ring and a society wedding as her right. In fact, thinking about it, she hadn't actually asked him for anything. She'd simply been there — fixing his computer, helping her grandmother, forgiving the man who'd wrecked her self-esteem over five years. She fed the chickens and the cats, minded Pixel, befriended Gregory, and still her wells of kindness overflowed, as she wanted to nurse those who were sick and suffering.

She was a beautiful woman, and a wonderful lover.

What the hell was he doing? Just because he'd set a plan in motion didn't mean he had to abide by it. So what if he'd got his grant to travel? If need be, he'd give it back. He'd find a place for Gregory and Banquo together, in Newcastle. And if that didn't work out, then too bad about writing books and being a literary success. He'd get an ordinary job and take care of his father, just as Cathy was planning to do for Nan.

He would stay, but would Cathy even consider loving him?

He loved her.

No, he hadn't said it. Not to any partner. Never once in his whole romantic life had he looked into the eyes of a woman and said with sincerity, 'I love you'. He was nothing if not honest. Nobody had ever touched his heart as Cathy had done.

Outside an ordinary house where roses bloomed in a garden bed and children were romping with a dog, David's steps slowed. 'Please hear me out, Cathy? I have something to say.'

She was looking at him fully for the first time today. Her clear blue eyes were questioning, her soft lips no longer so firmly set. 'Something to say?'

He nodded and told her everything, while her look of disbelief was gradually changing to one of hope. Yet her silence told him she was unconvinced.

'Don't you believe me?'

'I believe you. It's just . . . '

'Yes?'

'I think you're making this decision because of me. I don't want the responsibility, David. It has to be what you want. Tell me honestly — is it?'

He drew in a sharp breath. His options were to give up writing or abandon his father. Even without Cathy in the picture, he had to make an impossible choice.

At least she'd taken his words on

board and believed him. She slipped an arm through his as though accepting him back into her life. They turned for home, not needing to talk. The silent language of their renewed touch was enough.

Nan and Gregory were oddly quiet when they arrived. It was as though some private transaction had taken place between them. Apart from a little general conversation, the visit appeared to have run its course. David waved goodbye and went back to his father, needing time to process the day's events.

'Did you enjoy yourself, Dad?'

'I certainly did. Joy's one out of the box.'

'I could see you were getting along famously. I'll do the washing-up now.' As he stacked plates, he reflected on Cathy's words. He might have earned back her respect, but in reality he was no closer to a happy solution.

But a new factor emerged within two days. Gregory requested a return visit to the doctor, and emerged with a letter stating that, apart from limited vision, he was physically and mentally fit for his age. Nan advised her social worker that she had found a boarder to share her home, and was ready for discharge.

'You mean this was all decided in the space of half an hour, while we were out?' Cathy was incredulous, but her grandmother smiled.

'You act fast when thin ice is cracking under your feet.'

'But it's so impulsive! What if you don't get on together?'

'He'll be a boarder, with his own space. I love cooking; I don't mind feeding him. And he'll be there to get help, if I ever have another fall.'

'I don't think you've thought this through.'

'At my age, I can't make long-range plans. Day by day is how it goes. Think of that fire. Gregory was supposed to be in a place of safety and he's lucky that he got out alive.' She took Cathy's hand. 'Nothing's set in stone, dear. We can only try. And as soon as I'm discharged, I'm entitled to temporary assistance, a weekly cleaner, even Meals on Wheels.'

'You really intend to do this, don't you?'

'I want my little dog, and my animals. Banquo and Gregory will be a bonus. It can be lonely, living alone.'

'Yes.'

'Perhaps it's time to go and talk this over with your David. He's probably as surprised as you are.' Nan chuckled and, seeing the light of determination in her eyes, Cathy bent down and embraced her wily grandmother.

She rang David as soon as she stepped outside. 'I'm in the hospital car park. Has Gregory told you what he's planning?'

'We're discussing it now. His mind's made up. What on earth do you think about it?' He sounded as confused as she felt.

'Apparently the social worker thinks it's an acceptable arrangement.'

'Dad's got a doctor's letter. It's a bit sudden, don't you think? They don't know each other.'

'I know. The thing is, though . . . '

'Yes?'

'Is it really any of our business?'

'It is if I'm on the other side of the country and there's some crisis.'

But Cathy was silent for a moment, feeling the ties of responsibility falling away.

She felt a new future opening. With Nan and Gregory housed, she could sit down with David and discuss just what that might be.

'Why don't you come over this evening?' she suggested. 'We seem to have a lot to talk about.'

They arranged to meet later. Cathy felt compelled to walk off her new state of nervous anticipation and diverted to the beach, where she walked alone. She felt she was floating; a drop in some vast, ever-moving sea where life and love and death arose and disappeared. Beyond her control, but within her grasp, to accept what came to her with joy.

★　★　★

Why was David waiting for her? As she parked behind his car, she saw him sitting on the front steps, Banquo by his side. Surely she'd said 'this evening'? She had nothing for dinner. He would simply have to have a toasted sandwich if he was hungry.

Her hair was tousled, her skirt was crushed, and she had sand on her feet. David, on the other hand, looked as though he'd just sprung from the shower. In fact, he was quite formally dressed in dark trousers and a long-sleeved white shirt, open at the neck. He looked as though he was going to some special event. If so, he would have to go alone. Today had delivered enough surprises and the last thing she felt like was dressing up and being sociable with strangers.

'What a day!' she called, locking the

316

car and stooping to brush the sand off her bare feet. Carrying her sandals, she walked towards him, the breeze carrying a strong waft of his aftershave to her nose. Where was he going? He was wearing dress shoes and socks, for heaven's sake!

'Why are you all done up?'

He ignored the question. 'I've been waiting for you.'

'I can see that.' A flash of alarm struck her. He seemed rather serious. Surely nothing was wrong with Gregory? 'Has something happened?'

'I hope so.'

She looked at him blankly. Perhaps the news that Gregory and Nan intended to live together had thrown him off course. 'I know it's very sudden.'

'Sudden? Why do you say that?' Now he sounded worried.

'Well, they're virtual strangers. But Nan isn't expecting your father to propose!' She laughed at that idea. 'As companions, I think they will be quite well-suited.' She fumbled for her key, hearing Pixel's indignant yaps on the other side of the door. 'Poor little thing! She's been at home by herself all day. By the time I saw a client and went to the hospital . . . '

He seemed relieved as he sprang to his feet. 'Why don't you sit down and relax? I'll take her for a walk with Banquo.'

It was an unusual suggestion, but he sounded quite determined. And a short respite appealed. 'Thanks, David. I can have a quick shower while you're gone.' *And see what the rest of the day brings*. He was in a strange sort of mood. But she was beyond surprises. A touch of Nan's fatalism had rubbed off on her. What would be would be.

She was just out of the shower and pulling a comb through her wet hair when she heard the doorbell. Pulling on her bathrobe, she went to let him in, leaving damp footprints on the polished wood.

'You were quick!' She noticed in

surprise that Banquo was wearing his guide harness. 'Why has he got that on?'

'Retraining him for Dad. You take him. Close your eyes and let him lead you.'

If he wanted to play games, she didn't mind. She grasped the handle of the harness and Banquo obligingly stepped out while she shut her eyes, imagining how life would be if one's sight was gone. The bond with the dog was incredible. He trod with assurance, and she felt each step underfoot as though pacing down a long aisle. In the sitting room he directed her to the sofa and sat, as if to say, *Here we are!*

'Good boy!' Opening her eyes, she fondled his soft ears. Glancing up, she saw David progressing towards her, Pixel trotting at his side on her short lead. She seemed to have something attached to her small collar. David brought her to Cathy and the dog immediately jumped up on her lap.

'What's this then?' Cathy saw the

little message card. 'Is this a dinner invitation?'

'Read it and see.' His voice sounded nervous, strangely hoarse.

She opened the note and read the words.

★   ★   ★

Cathy, my darling, will you marry me?

★   ★   ★

Seven little words. The same way their relationship had started at the writers' workshop.

It wasn't supposed to be like this. But this time it was different. For it *was* supposed to be like this. He was the man of her dreams, the man she wanted to spend the rest of her life with.

'Oh yes. Yes please! I love you, David.'

'And I love you, with all my heart.'

Picking her up, ignoring her wet hair, dropping loving kisses on her neck, he carried her to the bedroom and lay her tenderly down.

This was true lovemaking. The sexual tide swirled in her blood, as it surely did in his.

He kissed and kneaded her pink nipples, sending shafts of strong desire deep into her pelvis. She felt her muscles clench and contract, her curves and folds grow damp with longing. He peeled the bathrobe from her bare skin, admiring her as though she was a precious work of art. Shedding his own clothes, he touched and stroked her body, his own arousal hard and urgent yet controlled, as though he wanted her to be sated with pleasure before he took his own.

Her movements were slow and languid as she stretched out beneath his caresses. She heard small moans, surely not his, for he was whispering endearments as he pressed his lips against her ear. She was unfolding; melting on this tide of want, pulling him close, moving with supple grace as she shifted to kneel facing him, taking her turn to run her hands across his strong chest, over his muscled shoulders and down his firm-boned back. He shuddered as her fingers crept lower, infinitely gentle as they reached his most sensitive, tender flesh.

In turn he fondled her, grasping her soft buttocks and feeling his way with assurance towards the center of her arousal. He kept kissing her, whispering to her. She could hardly hear the words. They didn't matter, for their tone expressed such deep love and sincere caring. For some reason, tears filled her eyes as she positioned herself against him and with an assertive push he slid home into her deepest being. This was love. Surely, combined with the exquisite intimacy they were sharing, she was feeling the highest expression any man and woman could find together. And she was lucky enough to share this with David, her soul mate, her lover and her future husband.

They lay entangled, too lazy to move

as heartbeats resumed their normal pace and their breathing settled. David raised himself to lean on one elbow, gazing down at her.

'I'll buy you a ring as soon as my next royalties arrive. Dad wanted to advance me a loan, but I'm going to do this by myself.'

'We can talk about it later. The main thing is we're together.'

'Does that mean you'll come with me to Broome? I'm leaving next week.'

She considered the idea, realizing every obstacle was miraculously wiped away. Nan and Gregory, the dogs, even the nursing course; for she'd just been advised she was eligible for the next intake. Before she began her studies, she and David could travel for several months before returning to Newcastle, in time to celebrate their wedding.

'A week!' She made a half-hearted effort to throw off the numbing relaxation that seemed to promise the future would take care of itself. 'How would I get Nan settled, and advise my customers, and deal with the lease — '

'Cathy, no lists!' He closed her lips with a kiss. 'We'll get everything done, I promise. Now, shall I make coffee?'

Lazily, she nodded. David opened the door and stood there, laughing. 'You must see this!' He beckoned and she went to look.

Like a pair of mismatched lovers, Banquo lay stretched out in the hallway, sound asleep, with Pixel nestled into his chest. Both dogs were snoring.

'Love's in the air,' David murmured, his gaze on her as he drank in her beauty. 'Coffee can wait.' And, quietly closing the door, he pulled her into his arms and led her back to bed.

*   *   *

It was surprisingly easy to facilitate Nan's discharge from the overstretched hospital system. Within days, a visiting physiotherapist and temporary home help were arranged, with the offer that

Meals on Wheels could be delivered if desired.

There was no mistaking Nan's delight when, carefully using her stick, she walked up her own garden path and inserted the key in her own front door. All Cathy's hard work was rewarded by the look on her grandmother's face as she examined the blooming potted plants and nodded at the sight of the chickens contentedly pecking around the yard. Like a bride in a brand-new home, she inspected every room, fingering new fabrics and sniffing the floral aroma drifting from the newly cleaned carpets.

The large spare bedroom had been made ready for Gregory. A new mattress and pillows had been delivered at his expense and David had replaced the clothes lost in the fire. Apart from Banquo and his gear, Gregory only wanted his radiogram and records, his medical regime and a few personal items. The doctor had passed him as mentally and physically fit but, given his diabetic history, he was to receive a regular visit from a community nurse.

This must be how parents feel when their children marry and leave home, decided Cathy. She and David had their private doubts that the elderly pair could manage, but their every concern was brushed aside.

'Do stop fussing, Cathy!' Their roles temporarily reversed, Nan spoke like a resentful teenager. 'All I need is someone to go for a daily walk with me, or to pick up the phone and ring the doctor if I have some mishap. All Gregory needs is sensible feeding and someone to tell him when it's time to use that diabetic pen. A dietician is coming to talk to us both. It's all under control.'

'But what about shopping? Laundry?'

'What century do you live in, child? Haven't you heard of the internet and home delivery? I'm not senile. I do know how to work the washing machine and the dryer. And in a couple of months I'll be able to drive again.'

Cathy had to agree that most issues seemed to be under control. Perhaps she was fussing too much.

'When are you bringing Pixel home?'

'Tonight, if you like.'

Though it would be hard, handing back the affectionate little dog she'd cared for.

★ ★ ★

The airfares were booked and paid for. Cathy's excitement as she perused the flight details was tempered by worry that she'd used most of her savings.

'I could have gone to London and back for the same fare!' she told Nan.

'Australia's a huge continent. That's why it's so diverse. I may have lived in Newcastle all my life, Cathy, but I watch documentaries. I travel in my head.' Nan pulled out a check and gave it to her granddaughter. 'This is my little thank you, for all you've done.'

The gift would cover the airfare and more. Cathy gave a gasp. 'You can't afford this.'

'Now you want to control my money as well as my life?' Nan laughed. 'We Virgos always have a nest-egg, don't we? You take that money and start living before it's too late. Gregory and I will try things out and see how we get along.'

How strange to think you could make a few simple phone calls and change your life.

Cathy had notified her customers, ended her lease and left her goods in storage. She'd posted back her acceptance of the nursing course. In twenty-four hours she and David would be on the coach to Sydney, to travel by a nine-hour direct flight to Broome.

David had simply locked up his apartment and his father's family home. There would be time enough to settle those affairs when he came back.

He'd advised Cathy to travel light. 'We may be hiking around the area, so pack what you can carry. We certainly won't need heavy clothing at this time

of year and we'll be home before
winter.'

★　★　★

The coach to Sydney was picking them
up at seven next morning. They had
said their farewells to their relatives.
Cathy carried away in her mind a
picture of Nan and Gregory waving
from the gate, the dogs at their sides.
Was it really possible to change course
this easily? To leave behind everything
that was your life, to start a new
adventure? What if it didn't work out?
No. She rejected that thought. With
David at her side, she knew that was
just the price you paid for falling in
love. You had to take a chance on love,
and trust.

Epilogue

The plane flew over skyscrapers and the harbor views of Sydney, touching down with a gentle jolt. Cathy, in the window seat, watched the busy terminus of Sydney airport at work. Grounded planes awaited takeoff or arrival procedures while laden baggage carts ran to and fro. It was hard to compare this industry to the unregimented recent months she'd spent with David.

The time had flown. Now it was time to readjust, and she wondered what they'd find back in Newcastle. Moving around so constantly in pursuit of David's research, she'd abandoned the idea of email and phoned Nan from time to time. Apparently all was going well.

'Ready?' David hoisted their overhead bags from the luggage carrier. She eyed the long, strong lines of his body and stood up slowly; reluctant to leave all the memories of their first months together as a couple. She'd decided they were born traveling companions. There hadn't been a single conflict as they explored Broome and the surrounding areas. They'd been able to visit the Djarindjin Community on the Dampier Peninsula. The people there had welcomed her and she'd had a first-hand opportunity to learn a little about their traditional way of life. She'd gone on walks to identify bush tucker and tried her hand at mud crabbing. While David sat with tribal elders, learning their stories of the area's pearling history, she'd snorkeled and gone swimming in the warm coastal waters, floating while the pure blue void above infused her with a weightless happiness.

'Let's pick up your luggage.'

David grinned. True to his word, he'd traveled light. But the day before, he'd watched Cathy wrestling to pack all her souvenirs — the mosquito net and coils, the tramping boots, the aboriginal dot painting, and presents for Nan and Gregory and the dogs. In the end, she'd accepted fate and gone out with him to buy a cheap suitcase.

Once they were processed by security and left the terminal, Cathy switched on her mobile phone, smiling at the photo of herself astride a surly-looking camel.

'I'm just letting Nan know we're on our way to Newcastle.'

David nodded, very content with the prospect of starting a new book and a new life with his bride-to-be.

Cathy had ended her lease and was free to move to his apartment as soon as they arrived. From there, the first port of call they arranged was to visit Nan and Gregory. She did not altogether trust her grandmother's glowing reports of her transition to living with David's father. The arrangement seemed fraught with difficulties, she'd thought, although David took a more positive view. He said that the fire at the nursing home had changed him. It seemed there was no absolutely foolproof way to avoid accidents and crises. Wherever you were, fate had a way of finding you.

'Let them sort out their lives,' he'd advised, hugging her when she shared her worries. 'Your nan says they're fine. We should believe her.'

Whatever doubts Cathy had were dispelled on their first visit to Sandgate. They were expected for lunch but arrived early, in time to see the couple on their way home from their morning walk. In the distance, Banquo was in his guiding harness, while Pixel was a scrap of bobbing fur. Gregory and Nan were arm in arm, apparently chatting and unaware they were being observed.

'She's walking normally.' Cathy sighed with relief. 'She says Gregory insists on going out, rain, hail or sunshine.'

'It's good for Dad, too. That was half his problem, just moping around the house by himself. Come on.' David put his arm around her shoulders. 'Let's go and report in.'

Nan had retained a regular gardener, and the flowerbeds were colorful with the last of the autumn marigolds.

'I realize I have to be sensible, Cathy. No more digging while I'm screwed together with pins!' She laughed, aware of her granddaughter's sharp eyes checking the contents of the fridge and the washing pegged out on the line. 'Gregory and I have worked out a way to share most tasks.'

Cathy saw chickens still pecking around the yard, but most of the cats were gone. 'You called the ranger?'

'Gregory made me see reason. The RSPCA said they could find homes for the kittens and I paid for a few of my favorites to be de-sexed and returned. It was a hard decision.'

'Of course, Nan. You did the right thing.'

'I was lucky. Gregory helped me share my grief.'

Inside, Nan indicated a pile of

redirected envelopes. 'I've kept them safe for you, dear.'

It only took a few minutes to crumple up the junk mail. In addition, there was a confirmation of acceptance into the next nursing intake, and a completely unexpected note from Aaron. The computer-generated text had a business feel, but he had tried to apologize.

My parents have helped me to understand your reasons for leaving, and I trust you will make a productive life. You may be assured that I will not pursue our connection any further. Regards, Aaron.

It might not be a warm way to confirm their relationship was over, but she understood it was the best that he could do.

Nan had made a sponge cake and sultana scones for lunch. The foursome sat around the old table where Cathy had regularly eaten so many years ago.

The same oilskin tablecloth was in place; the same china fruit bowl with its handle shaped like a banana. Banquo was at his master's side, his brown eyes fixated on the ever-diminishing scone in Gregory's hand. Pixel, more interested in attention than food, scrambled at Cathy's leg with her tiny paws, demanding a cuddle. David and his father were deep in conversation about the physiology of the bends, a pearl diver's hazard.

'The agonizing pain is caused by nitrogen dissolved in the blood,' informed Gregory. 'It causes pressure on the nerves. The old way to decompress was to send the diver back to a depth where the pain ceased, and bring him up slowly enough for the nitrogen to disperse.'

Nan, meanwhile, was telling Cathy about the fascinating walks through the local wetlands. 'The old swamp has been completely redeveloped,' she said. 'They've carted away all the rubbish and put paths through. We're going to tackle the circuit walk soon.'

As Nan talked about the ibis, egrets, pelicans and swans, Cathy relaxed. For now, this was a happy arrangement, and it was clear that Gregory and Nan had found a way to enjoy life together.

'We're doing all the talking,' she said. 'Now, what about you two? Happy?'

David smiled at her. 'Very. I plan to get my book written, but Cathy's decided to exchange her fiction-writing for study assignments.'

'We don't need two writers in the family,' Cathy confirmed. 'And once I start nursing, I'll have plenty of assignments to keep me busy.'

They hadn't made long-term plans, though David had suggested they could sell his apartment and move out of the city. And when that happened . . .

'One other thing — we're getting a puppy,' she said firmly, as David turned his surprised, admiring gaze on her, and Banquo's tail thumped approval.